Ed. Heckman 5/23/61

# BLANK VERSE AND CHRONOLOGY IN MILTON

*by Ants Oras*

UNIVERSITY OF FLORIDA PRESS / GAINESVILLE, 1966

EDITORIAL COMMITTEE

*Humanities Monographs*

T. WALTER HERBERT, *Chairman*
Professor of English

G. PAUL MOORE
Professor of Speech

CHARLES W. MORRIS
Professor of Philosophy

REID POOLE
Professor of Music

C. A. ROBERTSON
Professor Emeritus of English

MELVIN E. VALK
Associate Professor of German

AUBREY L. WILLIAMS
Graduate Research Professor
of English

PR
3581
.O7

---

COPYRIGHT © 1966 BY THE BOARD OF
COMMISSIONERS OF STATE INSTITUTIONS
OF FLORIDA

LIBRARY OF CONGRESS
CATALOG CARD No. 66-63667

PRINTED BY ROSE PRINTING CO., INC.
TALLAHASSEE, FLORIDA

## CONTENTS

| | |
|---|---|
| 1. Introduction | 1 |
| 2. Use of Adjectives and Adjectival Participles | 10 |
| 3. Milton's Use of Metrical Pauses | 24 |
| 4. Word Length | 31 |
| 5. Feminine and Pyrrhic Endings | 36 |
| 6. Conclusion | 38 |
| Notes | 41 |
| Graphs | 43 |
| Tables | 59 |
| Appendix | 83 |

# INTRODUCTION

THE FOLLOWING PAGES present a series of stylistic analyses, in the hope of, in some degree, clarifying the much obscured issue of the relative chronology of Milton's major poems—the internal chronology of *Paradise Lost* and the chronological positions in Milton's poetic output of *Paradise Regained* and *Samson Agonistes*. Concerning all of these, new theories have been suggested in the course of the last two decades. It goes without saying that without some certainty in regard to the order in which these works or their principal parts were written, no valid studies of Milton's development as a poet can be undertaken.

The most startling of the new theories are those which place the composition of *Samson*, or at least its beginnings, somewhere back in the 1640's, making it precede *Paradise Lost*. As far back as 1941, Harris Fletcher in his edition of Milton's *Poetical Works* suggested that the tragedy might have been composed in its general outlines "at almost any time after 1640, and slowly brought to completion between 1650 and 1670."[1] Somewhat later, in 1947, Allan H. Gilbert also assumed the tragedy to be early.[2] However, these were merely suggestions.

The most important arguments so far presented in favor of an early date for *Samson Agonistes* are those put forward by William Riley Parker in his article "The Date of Samson Agonistes" (*PQ*, XXVIII, 144-66). He pointed out the absence of any unassailable evidence for its position at the end of Milton's poetic career. The essential points he made are, briefly, as follows:

1. Even Milton's nephew, Edward Phillips, knew only that *SA* appeared in print together with *PR*, the poem "begun and finished after the other [*PL*] was published, and that in a wonderful short time considering the sublimeness of it." Parker interprets Phillips' statement as suggesting that he did not believe *SA* was composed after the publication of *PL*, that is, between the dates of 1667 and 1670, the years in which Phillips considered *PR* to have been written. "From 1667 to 1670 seemed to Phillips a 'wonderful short space' for the composition of the 2,070 lines of *Paradise Regained*. How much greater the wonder would be if, in the same space, Milton did compose the 1,758 lines of *Samson Agonistes!*"

2. Milton's attitude to rhyme as expressed in his prefatory note on "The Verse" is taken to constitute a "credo," making it unlikely that he shortly before or after such a statement should have used rhyme in SA.

3. The reading into SA of autobiographical references concerning the period after 1660 is attacked as uncritical. Parker finds no references which could not equally well apply to earlier periods of Milton's life. The prophetic attitude in the tragedy would, he considers, seem to fit better into the time when Milton's hopes for a collective regeneration of England had faded and he began to place his hopes only in the chosen few, that is, into the years 1648-54. "Neither *Paradise Lost* nor *Paradise Regained* contains such an emphasis; but the *Samson* contains it, reiterates it, and dramatically gives it illustration. Is there anything in Milton's life after the Restoration which can explain a revival of this conviction?"

4. The metrical experiments in the choruses and monologues of SA strongly recall the irregular Latin verse of "Ad Joannem Rousium," written in 1647. This was some years after the period when Milton, according to Phillips, contemplated dramatic composition. In 1645-48 he produced no pamphlets and "almost certainly returned to his idea of writing a tragedy." This was also a period when Phillips probably had finished his residence with Milton, so he may not have known of the work his uncle was engaged in at the time. Another period during which he may have been ignorant of the poet's occupations was 1664-65. At that time Phillips was tutoring John Evelyn's son at Sayes Court near Deptford.

5. 1646 or 1647, then, would be a likely time for Milton to have begun work on SA, to resume it in 1652 or 1653, with some thought of including it in a revised edition of his poems. Composition was probably discontinued in August, 1653, when he turned to translating psalms.

6. The translations of Psalms 80-88, done in April, 1648, when Milton's left eye had grown "dim and dead," are full of the agonized, angry spirit of SA. Those of Psalms 1-8, composed in August, 1653, contain strange, anarchic rhythms anticipating the form of the tragedy, and much of its spirit too.

7. Although Milton about 1640 had jotted down for dramatic treatment several topics dealing with Samson, neither these nor a number of later references to Samson show that emphasis on him

as the Hebrew hero, the "lonely champion who fought his country's enemies while 'his countrymen blamed him'" which appears in the *Defensio Secunda* and, of course, in the tragedy. Samson had become a subject for the type of tragedy that the poet wanted to compose. "We can believe that Milton felt little interest in Samson's attitudes until he, too, was a rejected champion facing the grim fact of blindness. This could hardly have happened much before 1647."

8. Samson's speeches on blindness have the touch of raw experience. Milton needed to express himself that way in order to achieve some kind of catharsis immediately after the staggering blow of blindness had fallen: "to write thus after the soul had found patience, after adjustment had been made, would surely be almost intolerable pain."

Such, as I see it, are the principal points in Parker's argument. Let us consider them one by one:

1. Edward Phillips' admission of not knowing when SA was composed may be understood as being just that—an admission of ignorance. The fact that *PR* took years to compose provides no clue concerning the speed with which *Samson* was written. The epic, essentially a carefully reasoned, meticulously finished *débat*, has little of the emotional force and momentum, the ring of profound personal involvement of the tragedy, which seems to me far more of a piece than it apparently does to Parker. The rate of composition may vary very greatly in the same writer. Goethe, for example, is known to have produced much of his work at improvising speed, although it took him a lifetime to finish his *Faust*, and although even some of his shorter works, for instance, his *Iphigenie*, required much planning and several rewritings before they were completed. Fifteen to twenty lines daily would have been enough to enable Milton to produce SA in a few months' time—sufficiently quickly for Phillips to have missed visiting him during its period of composition.

2. Milton's note on "The Verse" is perhaps not a "credo" but an outburst of anger at the readers who, according to the printer Simmons, demanded reasons "why the poem rhymes not." Milton, never a man to suffer fools gladly, is perhaps making rhyme the whipping-boy for his indignation, using something of the kind of language not infrequently encountered in his prose invectives. He

must have been deeply provoked by the failure of his readers to see the superiority of his blank verse to the monotonous glibness of so many of the rhymed couplets and quatrains which were becoming the accepted forms for the versifiers of those very years. The irony of it is that even *PL* has rhyme, but rhyme used unobtrusively, with unprecedented subtlety and skill.[3] In *SA* Milton again rhymes only intermittently, employing rhyme only as a means of special emphasis at points of stylistic culmination, very much in the manner of "the Italian poets of prime note" he mentions, who, having otherwise discarded rhyme, still used it in the lyrical passages of their plays, for instance, Tasso and Guarini.

3. There may be no justification for regarding *SA* as an autobiography in disguise, and it is perhaps true that the situation and the sentiments found in the play may fit earlier periods nearly as well as they fit the last years of Milton's life. But they do also fit the latter. Nothing, to be sure, is known of anything specific in those years to make the poet entertain hopes of a chosen one, a redeemer, a savior for the English nation. But were any specific reasons for such hopes needed? Like the prophets of old, Milton may have felt that what he regarded as utter wickedness could not last forever, that a change *had* to come. History has shown that if those were his feelings, they were not altogether unjustified.

4, 5. Milton, the master craftsman, always aware of all the resources of his art, and certainly never completely oblivious of any technical experiments he had made himself in the past, could easily have drawn on the latter even after the lapse of a couple of decades. I see nothing surprising in his doing again, rather differently and more perfectly, in the sixties of the century what he had done quite tentatively in a Latin ode in 1647. I have already discussed the problem of possible dates when he may have been working on *SA* without his nephew's knowledge. Poetry may be "fearfully and wonderfully made," as Parker rightly admits,[4] and there may be some truth in Milton's own reference to his "unpremeditated verse": not all of his work need be the result of "slow-endeavoring art."

6. The spirit of the psalms translated by Milton in 1648 and 1653 is of the kind that may have recurred to him during any part of his later years, which especially after the Restoration for a man of Milton's temper and persuasion must have seemed years of grievous humiliation, no matter how bravely he may have endured them. The rhythm of the translations of 1653 prepares us not only

for what we find in *SA* but also for the rhythmical boldness of *PL*, which, closely considered, abounds in rhythms whose unusualness and strangeness we do not realize because we have come to take the Miltonic style for granted, and also because the poet's control of them is so perfect.

7. The notion of Samson as a chosen champion doing the heroic work which the masses fail to do would seem to remain quite as apposite after the Restoration as before it. The poet here is depicting an ideal situation, one he hopes for with particular fervor because the times have become so black. Samson, "the rejected champion, facing the grim fact of blindness," as Parker puts it, is at least as much like the Milton of the Restoration as he resembles the Milton of 1647 or thereabouts.

8. Samson's speeches on blindness are harrowing indeed but they need not be expressive of "raw experience." The feeling behind them is powerful but it is transmuted into great art, much like the treatment of the same experience in the exordium to *PL* III. It had to be expressed with a maximum of power early in the tragedy to make the rest fully effective. Here, it would seem, Milton is doing what many great poets have done: not sparing himself, he is drawing inspiration from his own pain, thus, incidentally, also achieving a catharsis, for which there must have been some need even a decade and a half after the loss of his eyesight. I see a marked difference between the perfection with which he makes Samson utter his extreme despondency and the somewhat hectic, at times indeed anarchic, fashion in which he in places translated Psalms 1-8 in 1653. It is these pieces that seem to me to have been done under the stress of an agony which did not permit full artistic control even in translations: the feeling here seems "raw."

Parker's impressively organized and written essay performed an important service in calling attention to neglected aspects of Miltonic chronology. He asked pertinent questions. The problem is whether he found the right answers.[5]

The same issue of the *Philological Quarterly* which published Parker's article also contained one by Allan H. Gilbert, entitled "Is *Samson Agonistes* Unfinished?" (pp. 98-106) Gilbert finds weaknesses in the play. Ideas are introduced abruptly. Despite his condemnation in the prefatory note of "The Poets error of intermixing Comic stuff with Tragic sadness and gravity; or introducing trivial and vulgar persons," Milton is found to be doing these very things in his treatment of Harapha and Dalila. The use of widely scattered repetitive imagery and figures of speech is not considered to achieve the necessary degree of rhetorical effect. The Argument of the play is shown to differ in a number of ways from the actual contents of the tragedy. The conclusion reached by Gilbert is that SA may have been written "soon after the making of the notes [on plans for tragedies] in the Cambridge Manuscript." Something was needed in addition to PR to produce a sizable volume in 1670. "The poet thought of the old tragedy, had it bound, and turned it over to the bookseller."

It seems possible to agree with some of Gilbert's findings without drawing the same inferences. The widely dispersed figures of speech and images may not always immediately rise to the level of full awareness in the reader but they appear to be effective enough at a deeper level, not unlike the "iterative imagery" of Shakespeare analyzed by Caroline E. Spurgeon. The comedy in SA, as Gilbert later in the essay admits, is brought in "with discretion, and uncorruptly, not to gratify the people but to make the drama better," and it may be claimed, as the same essay suggests, that "the comic characters in Samson are not trivial, perhaps not even vulgar." This seems to answer Gilbert's own objections. There is some comedy also in PL, for instance, when the Prince of Darkness approaches Uriel in the disguise of a "stripling Cherube," or when he only a little later turns somersaults—"many an Aerie wheele"— winging his way down to Mount Niphates. Gilbert himself has pointed out touches of comedy in PR as well. One would consequently tend to conclude that a modicum of the comic element (which in Milton is mostly ironical or sarcastic) was not felt by the poet to be at variance with his conception of epic or tragic dignity.

What Gilbert has to say about the lack of finish in SA agrees at least as much with the assumption of relatively rapid composition as with Gilbert's belief in an early date. Moreover, the comparative roughness of Milton's manner in parts of SA seems essential to the effect of powerful spontaneity created by the work. To quote Douglas Bush: "The texture, it has been said, gives the Greekless reader a more authentic sense of the style of Greek tragedy than any translation of an actual play."[6] Too much polish, a too laborious application of the Horatian file might have seriously weakened the tragic impact.

The most elaborate attempt so far made to revolutionize Miltonic chronology is found in Gilbert's book on *The Composition of Paradise Lost*. Gilbert takes for his point of departure the lack of any positive knowledge concerning the order in which the parts of the poem were composed. He suggests that there may have been fundamental changes in its internal structure, citing instances of famous long poems which underwent much revision and recasting before reaching the state in which we know them. Among his examples are the *Aeneid,* Ariosto's *Orlando Furioso,* and Spenser's *Faerie Queene,* in regard to which he seems fully to accept Josephine Waters Bennett's theories. An even better example, well substantiated, would have been Goethe's *Faust,* in the case of which the labor of rearrangement, rewriting and insertion went on for the better part of the poet's long life, continuing almost to the day of his death and resulting in a work in many ways very different from the author's original intentions.

Making full use of what is known of Milton's early plans for a tragedy on the Fall and exploring also his notes for other, mainly biblical plays, Gilbert from parts of the epic constructs a hypothetical tragedy, much of which he thinks was actually put on paper. Then, he considers, Milton changed his mind, recasting his materials in the form of an epic, the events of which he first presented in straight chronological order, only later introducing the present, partly unchronological time sequence. In redistributing the parts of the poem, Gilbert divides most of the books of *PL* into sometimes very tiny sections—Book IV, for example, into twenty such segments, some of these consisting of only a few lines. In his final rearrangement he distinguishes six chronological groups. Group I contains matter "from the early Tragedies on the Fall (parts based on plans in the Cambridge Manuscript)." Group II consists of material "from other early tragedies," again "based on plans in the Cambridge Manuscript." Group III adds passages supposed to have been written for a final attempt at a tragedy. Group IV represents a stage of transition from tragedy to epic. Group V has matter "not suggested in the plans for tragedies and probably not planned until the epic form was settled on." Group VI completes the epic.[7]

A large part of Gilbert's reasoning is based on inconsistencies he finds between the poem and its Argument. Gilbert holds the Argument to be earlier than the poem; it is, he thinks, a preliminary outline according to which Milton worked, but from which he often departed in the later course of composition. He fails to consider the possibility that the Argument, as the Printer's note appears to suggest, may, like the note on "The Verse," have been mainly a contemptuous last-minute concession to unintelligent readers, perhaps dictated in some anger and not too carefully. Nor does he sufficiently take into account the not inconsiderable difficulties with which the blind poet was faced in consulting minor points in his text. Milton was a methodical man, but too laborious deference to those who manifestly formed no part of the "fit audience though few" to which he primarily addressed himself may not have been altogether to his taste.

There does not appear to be any need to go at this point into the details of Gilbert's argumentation. He cites enough reasons for his chronological suggestions to make his book appear not unimpressive at a first reading, although certain fundamental objections soon begin to assert themselves. The impression created by PL, no matter how many times one reads and rereads it, is essentially one of monumental unity. Douglas Bush considers it "a reasonable assumption, though some scholars would disagree, that Milton composed the poem mainly in its present sequence, for the sake of the imaginative momentum and structural ordering such a method would promote."[8] Besides, has Gilbert paid enough attention to the special situation in which Milton's blindness placed him? We know that he composed his epic mainly in the solitude of night when he had only his memory to rely upon for any parts of earlier work he may have wanted to make use of. Would not this almost unavoidably lead him to prefer fresh composition to the meticulous, mosaic-like piecing together of frequently very minor odds and ends suggested by Gilbert?

These and other considerations caused me to re-examine the chronological problem by subjecting Milton's blank verse to a series of consistently applied stylistic tests. In a lengthy paper on "Milton's Blank Verse and the Chronology of his Major Poems" (subsequently to be referred to as "Milton's Blank Verse")[9] I made an attempt to ascertain to what extent changes in style seemed to agree or disagree with the traditionally accepted chronological order. The features examined were: (1) pauses indicated in the original editions by punctuation marks other than commas; (2) the position of polysyllables in the pentameter line; (3) feminine endings—their frequency and phonetic nature; (4) the rhythmical type "Compleat Steel—Divine Property"; (5) syllabized -ed endings; (6) "pyrrhic" verse endings. Since most of these features will be dealt with again in greater detail and in larger contexts in the main part of this paper, all that needs to be said here is that from most of the tests a fairly well-defined pattern of development seemed to emerge. It often started with a sharp stylistic break between *Comus* and the early parts of *PL* and then usually continued to move still farther away from the masque up to a point midway in *PL*, whereupon its direction was slowly reversed, frequently leading to a situation resembling that in *Comus*, but with significant differences and with close links connecting *PR* and *SA* with the last books of *PL*. The conclusion drawn from these findings was that during the approximately twenty years that had elapsed since the composition of *Comus*, Milton had evolved a new style suitable for his epic purposes, to which he at first adhered with remarkable consistency but which he later somewhat toned down, resuming some of the practices which he, probably with varying degrees of deliberateness, had abandoned in the earlier books of the epic. The significant changes of style frequently occurring about the middle of the poem seemed to suggest some break in composition or some profound change in the poet's mood.

Some nine years later, in an article bearing the title "The Chronology of Milton's Major Poems" (*PMLA*, LXXVI, 345-58), J. T. Shawcross attacked the above conclusions. By a different arrangement of the same statistical data he attempted to prove the justification of Parker's and Gilbert's theories. Some of the matter included in my essay he passed over as irrelevant. Since his arguments will have to come in for some close examination in the main body of this monograph, they need not be dwelt on at present.

Shawcross also propounds a new theory concerning the date of *PR*. Having accepted the suggestions of Gilbert and Parker as valid, he on that basis arrives at the conclusion that *PR* consists of different chronological strata. Originally planned as a drama, which contained the main speech sections of Books I, II, IV, to which III was later added, it was, according to Shawcross, transformed into an epic by the addition of narrative parts and of passages in the speeches linking them with the narrative. Dramatic choruses were rewritten as narrative passages. The poem as a whole is regarded as, in large part, preceding *PL* as it now stands, but later than *SA*. As Shawcross' theory at its decisive points is dependent on the validity of the views of Parker and Gilbert, this is not yet the place for discussing it.

Two years after his article Shawcross brought out an edition of *The Complete English Poetry of John Milton (excluding his translations of Psalms 80-88) Arranged in Chronological Order* (New York University Press, 1963), in which *SA* is placed immediately before *PL*. The comments in this edition add nothing new on the problem of chronology.

# USE OF ADJECTIVES AND ADJECTIVAL PARTICIPLES

THE DATA PROVIDED in the tables and graphs for the present section include all adjectives used by Milton in his blank verse, and likewise all participles used in a strictly attributive function. Such usages as "that Forbidden Tree" or "lost happiness and lasting pain" are included, but not, for instance, the participles in "that happy State/ Favour'd of Heav'n so highly" or "Him haply slumbring on the Norway foam," where the verbal force in them comes strongly to the fore.

The categories into which the material has been subdivided are: (A) attributive adjectives and participles preceding the noun they modify—by far the most numerous type; (B) attributive adjectives or participles placed after the noun without becoming parts of a modifying phrase (e. g., "notes Angelical," "conjugal attraction unreproved"); (C) attributive adjectives (but not participles) following the noun as parts of such a phrase (e. g., "an Host/ Innumerable as the Starrs of Night"); and (D) all the rest, mostly adjectives used predicatively. Adjectival forms used substantivally ("the vast abrupt") or in a quasi-adverbial function ("God, who oft descends to visit men/ Unseen") are not included.

In this section, as throughout the present study, data are examined for *Comus* as a whole, for each book of *PL*, for each book

ADJECTIVES AND ADJECTIVAL PARTICIPLES

of *PR*, and for the non-lyrical parts of *SA*, which have been divided into three sections: (A) including the pentameters in the first two act-like subdivisions, lines 1-276 and 331-605; (B) those of the next two subdivisions, lines 721-1009 and 1061-1267; and (C) those in the final section, lines 1307-1744. The amounts of blank verse—474, 492, and 372 lines respectively—are just about large enough to be usable for our statistical purposes, whereas the first four "acts," taken individually, would have been too short. The divisions— Samson dejected, Samson roused, Samson preparing for, and then performing, his final feat—correspond to the main movements of the drama.

Alongside of the above data, I have also worked out the figures and percentages for *PL* subdivided into six groups of two books each: I-II, III-IV, V-VI, VII-VIII, IX-X, XI-XII, in order to bring out more distinctly dominant trends of development, and also to provide more exact parallels with Gilbert's groups, the number of which happens likewise to be six. The graphs, both in this section and elsewhere, are arranged in the way that seemed best for purposes of comparison: first, the graphs with the most detailed information; next, the abbreviated graphs, with *PL* subdivided into groups of two books; and finally, graphs with *PL* subdivided according to Gilbert's rearrangement.

There is continuity, definite shape, and logic in the graphs following Milton's own arrangement of his material. *Comus* is by far the most richly adjectival of Milton's major poems, but Books I-VII of *PL* also have a high, though steadily declining incidence of adjectives and adjectival participles. *PL* VII is followed by a steep drop. *PL* XII is very close to *PR* and *SA*. These two works, taken in their entirety, show almost identical percentages. A further point of interest is the scarcity of attributive adjectives (and participles) placed after the noun in *Comus*, followed by only a very gradual increase in frequency in *PL*, which culminates in *PL* VII, whereupon the curve in our graph slowly sinks to a level at several points only slightly above that of *Comus*. The important fact is that this decline is gradual and steady. *PR* and *SA* are in nearly all respects closely linked to each other and to the last books of *PL*. They participate to a marked extent in what has often been called the "bare," the unadorned style of the later books of *PL*. The increasing frequency of adjectival expressions in Books III and IV of *PR*— still not quite reaching the level of *PL* XI—can hardly have any

11

bearing on chronology. It is explainable on strictly functional and psychological grounds. Satan, having failed in his early attempts at persuasion, ever more urgently displays his rhetoric, the specious magnificence of what he is offering being demonstrated in an increasingly ostentatious manner. The technique adopted here is a deliberate crescendo technique. In *SA* the reverse is the case. There is of course intensification in the drama also, but it is not an intensification of oratory. While Samson still indulges in lamenting self-analysis, echoed and enlarged upon by the chorus, adjectives abound; as his determination grows and the tempo becomes sharper, the adjectival element subsides, to come briefly to the fore again in the final, quieter, more lyrically colored parts of the tragedy.

In contrast to the clarity of this picture, the graphs resulting from Gilbert's arrangement of *PL* make it difficult to discover any kind of clear pattern or internal logic. Nevertheless, *PR* and *SA* even here usually seem to be continuing some trend apparent towards the end of the curve for *PL*. They could not possibly be linked with *Comus*.

## *Syllabized and Unsyllabized -ed Endings (fixéd mind and fixt mind types)*

In "Milton's Blank Verse" considerable attention was paid to the treatment of participles and adjectives ending in -ed. My evidence has been criticized as irrelevant—quite erroneously, as I believe I shall be able to demonstrate, restating my case in a larger context than before.

The poetic device of syllabizing -ed endings where in ordinary speech the vowel had become mute was still very much alive in Milton's early days. It occurred most frequently when the ending happened to come between two stressed syllables, the accent of the adjectival (or participial) attribute and the initial stress of a noun (or sometimes another adjective). Poets of the Spenserian school in particular often used it also on other occasions. Giles Fletcher, for instance, frequently has such preterites as: carriéd, wateréd, depicturéd (all from *Christ's Victory on Earth*)—a usage which, however, occurs only once in Milton's earliest poetry: Poor fleshly Tabernacle enteréd ("The Passion," l. 17). Elsewhere he always avoids it, but the participle or adjective with the syllabized ending is a conspicuous characteristic of his early work. It continues to be used fairly freely in *PL* I-VII; then, however, it suddenly becomes exceedingly rare in the rest of the poem, and likewise in *PR* and *SA*.

These facts were pointed out in my essay as evidence that might be of significance for chronological purposes. Shawcross in his paper minimizes this significance. According to him, Milton "regularly syllabized '-ed' when the past participle had adjectival force, that is, when it appeared directly before the noun it modified" (p. 349). He produces examples from *Eikonoklastes* and other prose works. "The point," he says, "is simply that Milton frequently used the syllabized ending; it was not just a prosodic device" (*ibid.*).

The point, however, is by no means so simple. The syllabized ending certainly cannot have been a prosodic device in Milton's prose but there are differences between his attitude in prose and in verse. It is surprising that Shawcross fails to see any significance in Milton's avoidance of syllabized -ed endings in that very body of verse—everything from *PL* VII onwards—which normally has been regarded as the latest poetry he wrote—altogether some 9000 lines. It is at least equally surprising that a scholar who has specialized in the study of Miltonic spellings should not have noticed the existence of quite a number of instances in which the poet uses the parallel type with the unsyllabized ending in his early poetry. *Comus* alone has seventeen examples. Then, in the first half of *PL*, the number of such instances dwindles, to shrink close to zero (only one instance) in *PL* VIII-XII, to zero in *PR*, and to one isolated example in *SA*: a surprising parallel with the poet's use of the syllabized form.

Nevertheless, combinations of -ed attributes with nouns continue to occur—moreover, not infrequently. What changes when the normal arrangement would result in either the *fixt mind* or the *fixéd mind* type is the word order: the -ed form is placed after the noun. In the early poetry such inversions are exceptional. The early books of *PL* also have only relatively few examples, but thereafter the inverted order becomes the rule. When formerly Milton used phrases like: swink't hedger (*Comus* 293), wish't prey (*ibid.* 574), fam'd son (*ibid.* 1004), vex'd Scylla (*PL* II. 660), grievd look (*PL* IV. 28), or removéd place (*Il P.* 78), unownéd sister (*Comus* 407), singéd air (*ibid.* 928), wishéd Morn (*PL* I. 208), we now constantly come across such phrasal combinations as: Battles feign'd (*PL* IX. 31), som Orator renound (*PL* IX. 670), the Race of Mankind drownd (*PL* XI. 13), Queen ador'd (*PR* II. 212), a Prisoner chain'd (*SA* 7). It seems unreasonable to assume that this change could have been anything but deliberate.

The evidence is massive, but because of its importance for our purposes it is presented in full in the following lists, which in the section for syllabized -ed endings exclude only expressions where syllabization still remains common in ordinary speech.

### Syllabized -ed Forms

EARLY PERIOD. *Psalm CXIV:* froth-becurled head (8). *Psalm CXXXVI:* Amazed Heav'n (13), Golden-tressed Sun (29), horned Moon (32). *Nativity Ode:* hooked Chariot (56), armed throng (58), charmed wave (68), stringed noise (97), helmed Cherubim (112), usurped sway (170), arched roof (175), breathed spell (179), mooned *Ashtaroth* (200), sable-stoled Sorcerers (220), damned crew (228), youngest teemed star (240). *Death of a Fair Infant:* ycie-pearled carr (15), dearly-loved mate (24), low delved tombe (32), white-robed Truth (54), golden-winged hoast (57), præfixed seat (59), deserved smart (69). *Vacation Exercise:* piled Thunder (42). *On Shakespear:* piled Stones (2). *Solemn Musick:* undisturbed Song (6). *Circumcision:* winged Warriours (1). *L'Allegro:* loathed Melancholy (1), Ivy-crowned *Bacchus* (16), Wreathed Smiles (28), unreproved pleasures (40), lincked sweetnes (140). *Il Penseroso:* fixed mind (4), retired Leasure (49), fiery-wheeled throne (53), removed place (78), arched walks (133), heaved stroke (136), embowed Roof (157). *Arcades:* renowned flood (29), grosse unpurged ear (73). *Comus:* (Blank verse) unadorned boosom (24), mis-used Wine (47), charmed Cup (51), retired Solitude (376), unowned sister (407, abhorred rites (535), obscured haunts (536), unarmed weakness (582), uncontrouled worth (793), enraged stepdam (830), pearled wrists (834); (Lyrical verse) rushy-fringed bank (890), charmed band (904), insnared chastity (909), brimmed waves (924), singed air (928), crisped shades (983); (cancelled passage) removed climes. *Lycidas:* abhorred shears (75), beaked Promontory (94).

MIDDLE PERIOD. *Psalm LXXX:* Thy loved Josephs seed (4), tusked Boar (53). *Psalm LXXXIII:* their armed hands (31). *To*

ADJECTIVES AND ADJECTIVAL PARTICIPLES

*Cromwell:* crowned Fortune (5). *5th Ode of Horace:* changed Gods (6).
LATE PERIOD. *Sonnet "On His Deceased Wife"* (1658): my late espoused Saint (1). *Paradise Lost:* (1) *Book I:* many Throned Powers (128), fixed Anchor (206), wished Morn (208), singed bottom (236), inflamed Sea (300), linked Thunderbolts (328), Grazed Ox (486), fixed thought (560), armed Files (567), singed top (614), grasped arm's (667), arched roof (726), winged Haralds (752), squared Regiment (758), smoothed Plank (772). *Book II:* abhorred deep (87), Armed watch (130), ranged powers (522), obdured brest (568), Abhorred Styx (577), winged course (944). *Book III:* unapproached light (4), lapsed powers (176), incensed Deitie (187), winged messengers (229), fixed seat (669—twice in same line). *Book IV:* crisped Brooks (237), fringed Bank (262), unadorned golden tresses (305), unarmed Youth (552), winged Warriour (576), Espoused Eve (710), mooned hornes (978). *Book V:* winged Saint (247), winged Hierarch (468), Th' incensed Father, and th' incensed Son (844). *Book VI:* armed Saints (47), armed Peers (127), armed hand (231), deformed rout (387), orbed Shield (543), deserved right (709), Unfained Halleluiahs (744), helmed heads (840). Cf. also "light-armed scoure" (VI. 529). *Book VII:* winged Spirits (199), Arched neck (438). (2) *Book VIII:* droused sense (289). *Book IX:* no examples. *Book X:* forked tongue (518, 519). Book XI: winged Steeds (702), beaked prow (742), horned floud (827). *Book XII:* no examples. *Paradise Regained: Book I:* no examples. *Book II:* no examples. *Book III:* light armed Troops (311). *Book IV:* abhorred pact (191). *Samson Agonistes:* (Non-lyrical verse) armed powers (1190), armed guards (1617), arched roof (1634). (Lyrical verse) winged expedition (1283), perched roosts (1693).

UNSYLLABIZED -ED FORMS

EARLY PERIOD. *Death of a Fair Infant:* crown'd Matron (54). *Solemn Musick:* mixt powers (3). *Il Penseroso:* starr'd Ethiope Queen (19). *Comus:* (Blank verse) enthron'd gods (11), perplex't paths (37), vow'd Priests (136), swill'd insolence (178), swink't hedger (293), unsun'd heaps (398), unblench't majesty (430), congeal'd stone (449), lov'd masters heir (501), stray'd Ewe (503), wish't prey (574), damn'd wisard (570), curst crew (653), wing'd

15

air (730); (Lyrical verse) fam'd Son (1004), bow'd welkin (1015), wish't presence (950).

MIDDLE PERIOD. No examples.

LATE PERIOD. *Paradise Lost:* (1) *Book I:* fixt mind (97). *Book II:* fixt Laws (18), confus'd march (615), vex'd Scylla (660). *Book III:* glaz'd Optic Tube (590). *Book IV:* grievd look (28), faild Speech (357), unpierc't shade (245), wingd speed (788). *Book V:* fixt Starrs (176). *Book VI:* wisht houre (150), chaind Thunderbolts (589), forc't rout (598). *Book VII:* wav'd coats (406). (2) Only example in Book XII: Fixt Station (627). *Paradise Regained:* No examples. *Samson Agonistes:* Only example "feignd shifts" (1116).

-ED FORMS PLACED AFTER THE NOUN

EARLY PERIOD. *L'Allegro:* Daisies pide (75). *Comus:* the Tuscan Mariners transform'd (48), rod revers't (816).

MIDDLE PERIOD. *Psalm LXXX:* Meriba renown'd (32). *Psalm III:* men abhor'd (22).

LATE PERIOD. *Paradise Lost:* (1) *Book I:* Sulphur unconsum'd (69), Glory obscur'd (594). *Book II:* strict Laws impos'd (241), visage incompos'd (989), force renew'd (1012). *Book III:* peace assur'd (263), Angels disarraid (396), the Trepidation talkt (483), disembler unperceiv'd (681). *Book IV:* conjugal attraction unreprov'd (493), vapors fir'd (556), proud Steed reind (858), faith ingag'd (954), faithfulness profan'd (951), Satan allarm'd (985). *Book V:* Tresses discompos'd (10), Morn return'd (30), the Earth outstretcht (88), seraph wingd (277), shrub unfum'd (349), spirit accurst (874). *Book VI:* wrauth awak't (59), Helmets throng'd (83), look compos'd (469), branches lopt (575), Son belov'd (680), whole Legions arm'd (655), Angels arm'd (802). *Book VII:* Steed unrein'd (17), Chariots wing'd (199), Embryon immature involv'd (277), penaltie impos'd (545). (2) *Book VIII:* Adams doubt propos'd (64). *Book IX:* her nightly visitation unimplor'd (22), Battles feign'd (31), thoughts revolv'd (88), the Herd disguis'd (522), som Orator renound (670), of Death denounc't (695), after thoughts disturbd (918), these words constrain'd (1066). *Book X:* thy Son belov'd (70), Heavn and Earth renewd (638), Mind and Will deprav'd (825), this days Death denounc't (962), pleasure overlov'd (1019), the penaltie pronounc't (1022), his punishment ordain'd (1039), our Limbs benumm'd (1069), Sorrow unfeign'd (1092, 1104). *Book XI:* the Race of Mankind drownd (13),

ADJECTIVES AND ADJECTIVAL PARTICIPLES

Heavn and Earth renewd (66), warr unproclam'd (220), thy Lord appeas'd (257), life prolongd (331), God appeas'd (880), Man deprav'd (886). *Book XII:* the world destroy'd (3), world restor'd (3), joy unblam'd (22), Canaanite allarm'd (217), Laws ordain'd (226). *Paradise Regained: Book I:* my Son belov'd (85), The time prefixt (269). *Book II:* names ador'd (189), Queen ador'd (212). *Book III:* praise unmixt (48), a Lord confus'd (49), his foes pronounc't (120). *Book IV:* date prefixt (392), Son of God belov'd (513). *Samson Agonistes:* Prisoner chain'd (7), Hornets arm'd (20), coward arm'd (347), Nuptial Love profest (385), vows renew'd (520), words address (729), foe profest (884), of stock renown'd (1079), feats perform'd (1083), Some narrow place enclos'd (1117), a Man condemn'd (1224), a Slave enrol'd (1224), ears unus'd (1231), Favour renew'd (1357), a Nation armd (1494).

These lists show three distinct phases in the use of the three phrasal types. The early poetry manifests no aversion from either the *fixéd mind* or the *fixt mind* category but on only three occasions resorts to the third, inverted type. *PL* I-VII has all three, with the third type gradually gaining ground. After *PL* VII, the third type decisively predominates, almost completely ousting the others.

The evidence presents some further points of interest, already mentioned in my earlier study, but needing to be re-emphasized to make the picture complete. While the first half of *PL* has a considerable number of expressions with syllabized -ed occurring also in the earlier verse, in the second half of the poem, in *PR* and in *SA* the expressions repeated from the early poems nearly always have already appeared in *PL* I-VII (arméd, wingéd, abhorréd, archéd). Only the description of the Deluge in *PL* XI has two independent -ed links with the early work: beakéd (l. 746), with which compare *Lycidas* 94, and hornéd (l. 827), with which compare *Psalm CXXXVI* 32.

Very few of the expressions with the syllabized -ed found in my list after *PL* VI are new—altogether three instances: drouséd (*PL* VIII), forkéd (*PL* X), perchéd (*SA*). *PL* I-VI, on the other hand, has sixteen such forms: wishéd, inflaméd, thronéd, grazéd, graspéd, squaréd, soothéd in Book I; rangéd, obduréd in Book II; unapproachéd, lapséd, incenséd in Book III; deforméd, orbéd, light-arméd, unfainéd in Book VI. It is not without some significance that Book I has the greatest number of such new forms. This type, at

17

first still very much alive in *PL,* seems subsequently to have lost its vitality, surviving mainly in somewhat commonplace echoes from Milton's own recent work.

Since Shawcross' polemical article completely disregards the syllabized -ed parallels between the early work and the first half of *PL,* and since these parallels seem of some importance, I here repeat the list given in my earlier essay.

*PL* I: fixed (thought, anchor)—fixed mind (*Il Penseroso*)
singed (bottom, top)—singed air (*Comus*)
linked (Thunderbolts)—lincked sweetnes (*L'Allegro*)
winged (Haralds)—winged Warriours (*Circumcision*)
arched (roof), (*Nat. Ode*)—arched walks (*Il Penseroso*)
armed (Files)—armed throng (*Nat. Ode*)

*PL* II: abhorred (deep, Styx)—abhorred rites to Hecate (*Comus*); the blind fury with th' abhorred shears (*Lycidas*)
armed (watch)—see under *PL* I
winged (course)—see under *PL* I

*PL* III: winged (messengers)—see under *PL* I
fixed (seat)—see under *PL* I

*PL* IV: crisped (Brooks)—crisped shades and bowers (*Comus*)
fringed (Bank)—rushy-fringed bank (*Comus*)
unadorned (golden Tresses)—unadorned boosom of the Deep (*Comus*)
unarmed (Youth)—unarmed weakness of one Virgin (*Comus*)
winged (Warriour)—see under *PL* I
mooned (horns—of phalanx)—mooned Ashtaroth (*Nat. Ode*)

*PL* V: winged (Saint, Hierarch)—see under *PL* I

*PL* VI: helmed (head—of routed angels)—helmed Cherubim (*Nat. Ode*)
deserved (right)—deserved smart (*Death of a Fair Infant*)
armed (Peers, Saints, hand)—see under *PL* I
Note "armed hands" in *Psalm LXXXI* (1648)

What strikes one here is not only the number of syllabized -ed forms repeated from the early verse but also the fact that there is actual identity of expression in a number of the nouns, or otherwise close similarity of wording or context: fixéd thought (*PL* I)—fixéd mind (*Il P*); archéd roof (identical in *PL* I and *NO*); abhorréd

Styx (*PL* II)—abhorréd rites to Hecate (*Comus*); wingéd Warriour(s) (in both *PL* IV and *Circumcision*); fringéd Bank (*PL* IV) —rushy-fringéd bank (*Comus*); helméd head (of the fallen angels— *PL* VI)—helméd Cherubim (*NO*).

I quote my former comment, which I see no reason to modify (except perhaps for saying "Books I to VII" instead of "Books I to VI"): "This relative abundance of echoes would only seem natural if we agreed that Books I to VI of *PL* were the first substantial body of verse written by Milton since his early poems. Expressions from these poems, unobscured by much intermediate poetic composition, are likely in such a case still to have been alive in his mind. They would occur to him as he resumed the writing of verse. Sometimes they appeared with part of their context and sometimes not. They tended to appear in their original form, so long as this was compatible with the style which Milton wished to adopt, i.e., in the above cases with the fully pronounced ending -ed. This impulse and these associations then wore off. This was especially likely to be the case if a prolonged break occurred in the process of composition—particularly if it were a break filled with harassing experiences, such as the collapse of the Commonwealth and the restoration of the Stuart monarchy, with the resulting danger to the poet. The old associations thereafter reappeared mainly as echoes from the latest verse composed by Milton, that is, the first half of *PL*, rather than from his early verse, the continuity of association with which was broken."

## Types "Supreme Throne—Divine Property" and "Throne Supream—Lineaments Divine"

The above two types—likewise discussed in my earlier study, and likewise dismissed as unimportant by the same critic—will have to be re-examined here with a fuller presentation of the evidence in Milton.[10] The former of these patterns—an adjective (or participle) usually accented on the last syllable, followed by a noun with initial stress, and so placed that its stressed last syllable occupies a normally unstressed metrical position—is of course by no means uncommon in Renaissance verse, and even much later poets use it. Milton's feelings in regard to it appear to have changed in the course of his career. In his early verse this type of phrase is not infrequent. I find at least fifteen instances of it, fourteen of these in

Comus. PL I-IV has ten examples, but after PL IV there are only three possible instances (upright beams in PL VI. 82; adverse legions in PL VI. 206; adverse blast in PL X. 701).

Whatever one may think of Robert Bridges' suggestion that this type was being gradually discarded by Milton because it seems to have caused some rhythmical uncertainty,[11] the fact remains that where Milton might have used it after PL IV, he always, except for the instances mentioned, proceeds exactly as in the case of the *fixt mind–fixéd mind* types, that is, he inverts the order of attribute and noun. The early poems have only four examples of such an inversion. I present lists of both categories. It will be seen that many inverted -ed phrases belong here as well.

ATTRIBUTE PRECEDING THE NOUN

EARLY PERIOD. *Nativity Ode:* unshowr'd Grasse (215). *Comus:* serene Ayr (4), enthron'd gods (11), perplex't paths (37), Supreme good (217), extreme shift (274), compleat steel (421), unblench't majesty (430), unlaid ghost (434), congeal'd stone (449), unchaste looks (464), divine property (469), unjust force (590), unsought diamonds (732), sublime notion (785).

MIDDLE PERIOD. No examples.

LATE PERIOD. *Paradise Lost:* (1) *Book I:* unblest feet (238), obscene dread (406), supreme King (735). *Book II:* obscure wing (132), Supream Foe (210), unknown Regions (443), unknown dangers (444), confus'd march (615). *Book III:* oblique way (564). *Book IV:* unpierc't shade (245). *Book VI:* upright beams (82), adverse Legions (206). (2) *Book X:* adverse blast (701). *Paradise Regained:* No examples. *Samson Agonistes:* No examples.

ATTRIBUTE FOLLOWING THE NOUN

EARLY PERIOD. *Il Penseroso:* Troy divine (100). *Solemn Musick:* Hymns devout (15). *Comus:* the Tuscan Mariners transform'd (48), Knot-grass dew-besprent (542).

MIDDLE PERIOD. *Psalm III:* men abhor'd (22). *Psalm VII:* Judge severe (43).

LATE PERIOD. *Paradise Lost:* (1) *Book I:* Sulphur unconsum'd (69), Glory obscur'd (594), rest entire (671), shapes immense (790). *Book II:* Lord supream (236), Laws impos'd (241), custody severe (333), void profound (438), pomp Supream (510), Air

## ADJECTIVES AND ADJECTIVAL PARTICIPLES

sublime (528), a Fleet descri'd (636), void immense (829), Tartarus profound (858), visage incompos'd (989), force renew'd (1012), Spirits perverse (1030). *Book III:* drop serene (25), face divine (44), Spirits elect (136, 360), doom severe (224), love divine (225), peace assur'd (263), Joy entire (265), Head Supream (319), Spirit maligne (553), body opaque (619), Spirit impure (630), countenance triform (730). *Book IV:* debt immense (52), field secure (186), looks Divine (291), Eye sublime (300), leer maligne (503), light prepar'd (664), faith engag'd (951), name of faithfulness profan'd (951). *Book V:* Tresses discompos'd (10), Morn return'd (30), Fruit Divine (67), lineaments Divine (278), shrub unfum'd (349), thought infirme (384), love entire (502), Throne supream (670), Lightning Divine (734), zeale severe (807), birth mature (862), spirit accurst (877). *Book VI:* seat supream (27), wrauth awak't (59), Majestie Divine (101), fighting Seraphim confus'd (249), look compos'd (469), Entrails unlike (517), Son belov'd (680), Rayes direct (719), happiness entire (741), mighty Seraphim prostrate (841). *Book VII:* Voice divine (2), this flying Steed unrein'd (17), seat of Deitie supream (142), Spirits maligne (189), Majestie Divine (195), World unborn (220), matter unform'd (233), Darkness profound (233), ridge direct (293), th' air sublime (421), smallest Lineaments exact (477), Front serene (509), God Supream (515), the penaltie impos'd (545). (2) *Book VIII:* thoughts abstruse (40), doubt propos'd (64), Angel serene (181), shape Divine (295), presence Divine (314), voice Divine (436), Colloquie sublime (455). *Book IX:* venial discourse unblam'd (5), thoughts revolv'd (88), many a round selfrowld (183), Faith sincere (320), trial unsought (370), tract oblique (510), Herd disguis'd (522), som Orator renound (670), Death denounc't (695), good unknown (756), Fruit Divine (776), thoughts disturb'd (918), words constraind (1066), Adam severe (1144). *Book X:* strength entire (9), Entrance unseen (21), Throne Supream (28), Thy Son belov'd (70), Mole immense (300), Gulf obscure (366), Fate supreame (480), Heav'n and Earth renewd (638), Synod unbenigne (661), Ancestor impure (735), Mind and Will deprav'd (825), Justice Divine (857, 858), love sincere (915), this days Death denounc't (962), Race unblest (988), pleasure overlov'd (1019), the penaltie pronounc't (1022), his punishment ordain'd (1039), Limbs benumm'd (1069), Air attrite (1073), hearts contrite (1091, 1103), sorrow unfeign'd (1092,

1104). *Book XI:* Heav'n and Earth renewd (66), Throne supream (82), Warr unproclam'd (220), thy Lord appeas'd (257), Presence Divine (319), life prolong'd (331), track Divine (354), fit moulds prepar'd (571), Band select (646), World perverse (701), eyes devout (863), God appeas'd (880), Man deprav'd (886). *Book XII:* world destroy'd (3), world restor'd (3), objects divine (9), joy unblam'd (22), words unknown (55), a land unknown (134), blood unshed (176), Race elect (214), Canaanite allarmd (217), Laws ordaind (226), day entire (264), the Law of God exact (402), Goodness immense (469), the hour precise (589), air adust (635). *Paradise Regained: Book I:* voice divine (35), Son belov'd (85), time prefixt (269), truth foretold (453). *Book II:* pow'r unjust (45), Graces divine (138), names ador'd (189), Queen ador'd (212). *Book III:* judgment mature (37), praise unmixt (48), herd confus'd (49), times obscure (94), death unjust (98), foes pronounc't (120), things adverse (189). *Book IV:* Stoic severe (280), date prefixt (392), Son of God belov'd (513), Air sublime (542). *Samson Agonistes:* Nuptial love profest (385), vows renew'd (520), words address (729), foe profest (884), stock renown'd (1079), feats perform'd (1083), man condemn'd (1224), Slave enrol'd (1224), ears unus'd (1231), Favour renew'd (1357), sense distract (1556).

The picture presented by the above lists agrees very closely with that which we found in examining the evidence for -ed forms. A usage characteristic of Milton's early period and still surviving in the earlier parts of *PL* is later almost completely replaced by another linguistic habit, which from a rhythmical point of view usually produces exactly the same results as the postposition of the -ed adjectives and participles, many of which actually belong here.

Epithets placed in the normal way in the early poems often change their position in the later verse. In the early verse we have, for instance: Supreme Throne, enthron'd Gods, serene Ayr, compleat steel, sublime notion, divine Property, divine sounds, unjust force, unsought diamonds. Later we find the identical epithets placed after their nouns, sometimes the same nouns as in the early work: Throne supream (*PL* V, X, XI), pomp Supream (*PL* II), seat supream (*PL* V), God enthron'd (*PL* V), Angel serene (*PL* V), drop serene (*PL* III), Front serene (*PL* VII), look serene (*PL* X), King compleat (*PR* IV), Air sublime (*PL* II, VII, *PR* IV), harmonie Divine (*PL* V), pow'r unjust (*PR* II), death unjust (*PR* III), trial unsought (*PL* IX). The consistency with which this shift in position occurs suggests very deliberate usage.

As the above evidence indicates, the earlier parts of *PL* show greater variety in their handling of the patterns discussed than either the early verse or the verse commonly considered later—a fact agreeing with one's impression of the unique epic magnificence, the elaborately achieved heroic splendor of precisely this section of Milton's poetic output.

What may have caused these changes in Milton's usage? One point seems clear: he is moving away from Elizabethan and early Jacobean poetic conventions. In his early poetry Milton is still an Elizabethan. He uses what the late C. S. Lewis called "the golden style"—ornamental, rich in epithets, deliberately poetic, often original and subtle, but for all that still part of a prevalent tradition which he accepts and develops. He fully avails himself of traditional emotional associations in the choice of his devices. This style still has much of Spenserian "mellifluousness." The rhythmical smoothness secured by means of syllabized -ed endings is a case in point. By the time he is writing *Comus*, however, Milton seems already to feel the occasional need for more abrupt rhythms, supplied *inter alia* by his use of clashing stresses, as in the *fixt mind* pattern, and perhaps also in the *perplext paths—compleat steel* type, unless we assume a distinct recession of stress. In the course of his composition of *PL* his attitude towards gorgeousness of expression undergoes a gradual change. Discarding old conventional devices, he creates conventions of his own, more austere and farther removed from the accepted poetic habits of the time. This is the so-called "bare" style of Milton—not really bare, certainly not drab, for it has its subtleties, but many of these are not "poetic" by prevalent Elizabethan standards: the "Spenserian" element in Milton —some of which may have come to him from the Italians, as, among others, F. T. Prince has shown[12]—is reduced to a minimum.

## Non-Monosyllabic Adjectives Placed After the Noun

Another tendency taking Milton farther away from common Elizabethan poetic usage is observable in his attitude towards monosyllabic and non-monosyllabic adjectives placed after the nouns they modify. His early work decidedly prefers monosyllables in this position. I find only seventeen exceptions—somewhat less than seventeen per cent of the total. This is in keeping with a widespread Elizabethan habit, especially among poets writing in the Spenserian tradition. The reason for this preference may at least in part lie in the ballad-like, homely but poetical ring of this often slightly archaic usage. Compare, for instance: And what wul ye leive to your ain mither deer ("Edward"); my merry men all ("Sir Patrick Spens"); Until they came to a garden green ("Thomas Rymer"), With fifteen hundred bowmen bold ("Chevy Chase"). We hear the same tone in Spenser's: battell brave (*FQ* I. i, st. 3), her palfrey slow (*ibid.*, st. 4), sole king of forrests all (*ibid.*, st. 8); and likewise in Milton's: winter wilde (*Nat. Ode* 29), Olive green (*ibid.* 47), such musick sweet (*ibid.* 93), a daughter fair (*L'Allegro* 23), Barons bold (*ibid.* 119), inchantments drear (*Il Penseroso* 119). The longer forms, which especially in this position sound much less lyrically naïve and intimate, possibly for this reason begin to appear more frequently only in *PL*, particularly toward its middle and in the later books.[13] Their ratios—per 100 adjectival forms in this position—are as follows: *PL* I—48.7; II—58.5; III—53.3; IV—53.4; V—65.3; VI—73.5; VII—83.3; VIII—78.3; IX—60.2; X—71.3; XI—70.0; XII—79.1; *PR* I—68.0; II—64.5; III—60.0; IV—60.6; *SA* 67.9. After *PL* IV, the percentages for the longer forms never fall below sixty—one more item supporting the view that this part of Milton's work was composed later.

# MILTON'S USE OF METRICAL PAUSES

THE PRESENT STUDY of Milton's metrical pauses is based on the punctuation found in the original editions of his poems. It has been objected that for a study of pauses in verse, an examination of punctuation marks and their arrangement is "highly suspect." An evaluation "of each line according to meaning and syntax" has been considered a surer means of arriving at correct results.[14] Such an attitude ignores the considerable subjective element inevitably entering into such evaluations and disregards the fact that Renaissance punctuation by no means exclusively, and sometimes, indeed often, not even primarily, follows syntax or meaning in the manner present-day punctuation is intended to do. At least since Percy Simpson's pioneer studies, it has been clear that rhythm, the way verse *qua* verse was meant to be read, figured prominently among the considerations guiding Renaissance "pointing" in England. My own findings in my monograph *Pause Patterns in Elizabethan and Jacobean Drama* (University of Florida Press, 1960) fully corroborate this view. What becomes apparent from the statistical tables and graphs for a large number of works in that study is above all that Renaissance punctuation expresses patterns of rhythm, emerging distinctly even when the punctuation is careless and scanty; and also that these rhythms to a high degree reflect chronology. There is some reason to suppose that Shakespeare was not particularly concerned about punctuation. Nevertheless, even a superficial glance at my graphs for his works—quite especially those representing all punctuation marks, not only the strong ones—shows a striking degree of correspondence between the development in his treatment of pauses and the sequence in which his plays now fairly generally are believed to have been composed—not an absolute correspondence, of course, but a very close one.

Milton, methodical and scholarly as he was, can hardly be supposed to have failed to do his best to save his texts from remaining at the printer's mercy. That he was not indifferent to matters of punctuation, would seem to appear, for instance, from Edward Phillips' incidental remark on the problem when he speaks of having read *PL* "from the very beginning, for some years, as I went from time to time to visit him, in a parcel of ten, twenty, or thirty verses, which, being written by whatever hand came next, might possibly want correction as to the orthography and pointing."

We know from corrections of errata that orthography of a strictly individual kind received even the blind Milton's keen attention. It would be unreasonable to assume that "pointing," which Phillips specifically mentions, was ignored by one of the greatest and most careful masters of rhythm in the language, even though it may be taken for granted that not all his intentions in this respect were realized. It would seem even more strange to assume that Milton, while he still had his eyesight, did nothing to secure the right punctuation. The fact, referred to by Shawcross, that the Trinity College Manuscript has few punctuation marks seems of little weight, for it is obvious that no part of that manuscript represents Milton's text in the form in which it was intended to go to the printer.[15]

Consequently, the present study again faithfully follows the punctuation of the original editions. In this study *all* punctuation marks, including commas, have been taken into account.[16] My tables list the data: (1) for all punctuation marks; (2) for commas only; (3) for punctuation marks stronger than commas, that is, all the rest. It will be found that there is more continuity of development in the use of commas than in the more emphatic punctuation marks —partly, no doubt, because there are more of them, which makes them more reliable statistically, but also because they were probably placed more instinctively, with less deliberation: the poet's attention must have been focused more purposefully on the heavier pauses indicating the larger subdivisions of rhythm and meaning than on the lighter rests in the verse.

Two different sets of percentages have been worked out for these data: first, the incidence per number of lines; second, the percentages indicating the frequencies of the different categories of pauses viewed only in relation to each other, regardless of the number of lines in the work, or part of a work, in which they occur—the procedure adopted in my *Pause Patterns*. The latter set of percentages reveals regularities obscured especially in those cases where the frequencies, calculated per number of lines, were too slight to provide any distinct patterning in the graphs.

Like most English blank verse, that of Milton always concentrates most of its internal pauses into the middle of the line. Of the nine possible internal positions, the fourth and the sixth invariably have the highest incidence of punctuation marks; these, and the fifth position, taken together, are indicated in my tables and graphs by the Greek character $\mu$, whereas the rarer internal pauses at both ends of the line—the "extreme" pauses—are represented by the symbols $e^1$ (for positions 1, 2, and 3) and $e^2$ (for positions 7, 8, and 9).

The pentameter line readily falls into two halves of equal length, with the fifth pausal position placed in its exact middle. The symbol for the latter used here is *m*, that for the pauses preceding it, *a*, and for those following it, *b*.

Significant changes take place in the relative frequencies of pauses in the two half-lines, although Milton's later work never makes one half predominate over the other to anything like the extent found, for instance, in many Elizabethan pause arrangements. In the graphs given in my *Pause Patterns* the fourth pausal position often towers like a monstrously exaggerated Gothic spire, dwarfing everything else.[17] Even in the case of Spenser, one of whose most effective rhythmical innovations consisted precisely in his reducing this predominance of the fourth position, the long series of graphs for *The Faerie Queene* seems to be riding along like medieval knights with their fourth-position lances high up in the air. Figure III provides some points of reference, showing how marked the tendency of Milton's verse towards pausal equilibrium is if compared with the pentameters of many earlier poets. In this respect, *PL* comes close to the pause patterns in the plays which Shakespeare wrote about 1600, before the period of his most overwhelming emotional emphases, for instance, *Hamlet*, *Troilus and Cressida*, and *Othello*. Even so, Milton at no point has quite that evenness of pause distribution which makes the graphs for Ben Jonson so flatly rounded and low: his pausal emphases, balanced as they are, remain very distinct.

A look at the top sequence of graphs in Figure IV, which represents all pauses, both the internal and the final ones, shows a distinct overall trend towards higher frequencies from *Comus* through *PL* IX. Up to that point the curve rises with but minor descents on the way—the deepest in *PL* VI—but after *PL* IX the movement is downward, with *PL* XII placed at a point only slightly above *PR* I. The relatively steep rise from *PR* I to *PR* II is followed by an almost level plateau, sloping down in the later sections of *SA*. In the second, abbreviated graph of the same series nearly all uncertainties of direction have been evened out in the rising curve from *PL* I-II to *PL* IX-X, and *PR* and *SA* appear on exactly the same level, only two units above the end of *PL*. The same overall pattern, with only minor variations, is repeated in the graphs for commas. The graphs for strong punctuation, where the low figures make the contrasts much less noticeable, all along show a slow but rather steady progression away from *Comus*.

The dominant pattern here—an initial movement away from *Comus*, followed in the lighter pauses by a gradual movement in the opposite direction—agrees with the conclusions arrived at in "Milton's Blank Verse": a special style adopted for *PL* is carried to a culmination, but loses some of its distinctive characteristics in the later parts of the poem, in *PR* and in *SA*. The distances between pauses keep narrowing throughout three-fourths of *PL*, whereupon they again widen until the end of the curve.

What this implies is seen more distinctly as we proceed to

Figures V and VI, where the internal and the final pauses are represented by separate curves. The marked increase in the total frequencies of pauses is seen to be due mainly to the pauses within the pentameter line, whereas the incidence of line-end pauses in *PL* increases only very slightly, staying far below the internal pauses until *PR* II, whereafter it maintains a fairly steady level except at the end of *SA*, where the two curves meet. Milton's run-on technique, dominating most of *PL*, is eventually relaxed; well-marked final pauses become more frequent, at the end of the curve as frequent as pauses in the interior of the line.

The regularity with which these changes take place is most clearly observable in Figure VI, where only the relation between internal and final pauses is considered, the number of lines in which they occur being left out of account. Especially in the comma pauses the rhythm of change in *PL* is so even as almost to create the impression of having been expressly designed by a mathematician. In the graph for heavy punctuation marks, on the other hand, there is much less regularity of development. Trends which become very pronounced in *PR* and *SA* are only slightly adumbrated in the later parts of *PL*. The strong pauses throughout tend far more perceptibly towards the end of the line than the lighter pauses: despite his acknowledged practice of keeping "the sense variously drawn out from one Verse into another," Milton clearly felt the need for a sufficient number of sharply marked line-end rests to keep the main sections of his text distinctly separate. Only in some of the earlier parts of *PL*—most of all in Book II—does his taste for enjambment in a pronounced fashion affect his use of heavy punctuation marks, making him place a majority of them within the line.

The graphs showing the frequencies for pauses in the first half ($=a$), the second half ($=b$), and the middle ($=m$) of the pentameter line confirm the impression concerning the order of composition received from the graphs just discussed (Fig. VII). The graphs for heavy punctuation marks here show too little variation to permit any conclusions, but in those for all punctuation marks and for commas we find a repetition of the familiar picture of a movement first away from, and then slowly back towards, the situation in *Comus*. Only if the gradual nature of the changes in *PL* and the closeness of the later parts of the poem to *PR* and *SA* were to be disregarded, could one conceivably arrive at the conclusion that *PR* and *SA* precede *PL*.

METRICAL PAUSES

PR and SA remain closely linked in all graphs, except in the graphs for heavy punctuation marks in Figure XI. Here we find $e^1$ and $e^2$ much farther apart in SA than in PR, the extreme pauses in the tragedy tending more decisively towards the final third of the line. This may seem surprising, since extreme pauses late in the line usually go together with an intensified use of enjambment, which, as we have seen, is not the case in SA. A closer examination of the text suggests, however, that this peculiarity may be connected with the special staccato rhythm characteristic of much of Samson, the work with the highest incidence of heavy punctuation marks in Milton's blank verse. The sense in Samson is relatively seldom "drawn out" from line to line for any length of time; in this respect, the contrast is particularly sharp with most of PL (but also with Comus). Compare such passages in the drama as the following: "how well/ Are come upon him his deserts? Yet why?" (205); "but I my self,/ Who vanquisht with a peal of words (O weakness!)" (235); "the gold/ Of Matrimonial treason: so farewel" (959); "I know your friendly minds and—O what noise!" (1508); "Wearied with slaughter then or how? explain." (1583); "Mess. By his own hands. Man. Self-violence? what cause" (1584). Even enjambment here shows a tendency to appear in brief phrases or abrupt parenthetical insertions splitting the text rather than adding to its continuity: "(of the most/ I would be understood)" (191); "(which was worse/ Then undissembled hate)" (399-400); "yet if tears/ May expiate (though the fact more evil drew" (735-37); "I thought/ Gives and the Mill had tam'd thee? O that fortune" (1092-93).

Such rhythms are part of that very abruptness, or even breathlessness, of manner which elsewhere in the tragedy makes Milton produce conspicuous accumulations of asyndeta: "Besides, how vile, contemptuous, ridiculous,/ What act more execrably unclean, prophane?" (1361-62); "ev'ry sort/ Of Gymnic Artists, Wrestlers, Riders, Runners,/ Juglers and Dancers, Antics, Mummers, Mimics" (1323-25); "when all men/ Lov'd, honour'd, fear'd me, thou alone could hate me,/ Thy Husband, slight me, sell me, and forgo me" (938-40).

The angry choppiness of this style is poles apart both from the slow luxuriance apparent in much of Comus and from the irresistibly progressing, measured grandeur of the earlier books of PL. Some parallels to this manner, however, appear in the later, "barer" parts of the epic, notably in Adam's lonely lamentation in Book X, the desperately exclamatory style of which is exceptional in that book for its frequency of heavy internal pauses, particularly such close to line end:

> but his thanks
> Shall be the execration; so besides
> Mine own that bide upon me, all from mee
> Shall with a fierce reflux on mee redound
> (736-39)
> who knows
> But I shall die a living death? O thought
> Horrid, if true! yet why?
> (787-89)
> But say
> That Death be not one stroak, as I suppos'd
> (808-9)
> On mee, mee only, as the sourse and spring
> Of all corruption, all the blame lights due;
> So might the wrath. Fond wish!
> (831-34)

The dramatic manner of Samson's self-accusations is powerfully anticipated here as regards both tone and metrical technique.

Most of Milton's internal pauses occur in the even positions 2, 4, 6, 8, that is, at the end of disyllabic verse feet, the vast majority of which are iambic; in other words, most of his pauses follow a metrically stressed syllable, they are masculine pauses, more vigorous than pauses following a syllable without metrical stress (Fig. XII). The ratio of pauses in odd positions at only one point, in *PR* III, exceeds forty per cent. In *Comus* the percentage is less than thirty, and only in Books I and XII of *PL* is it over thirty-five. Then, in *PR*, it rises. The average for *PR* is the highest in Milton's blank verse, with *SA* a close second. It is to be noted, however, that in the tragedy the frequency drops off as the play progresses—rather sharply towards the end: as the mood of decisiveness grows and the dramatic tempo becomes more vigorous, the curve for the odd pauses declines—but, interestingly enough, not in the graph for heavier punctuation marks: here the curve for the odd positions at first rises. This balancing, as it were, of light masculine with strong feminine pauses—the latter of course much less frequent—occurs in a marked fashion at only two other points in our graphs, in *PR* I and II: another item linking these two works. None of the graphs representing the various aspects of Milton's treatment of pauses suggests the likelihood of any other chronology than that traditionally accepted. The least degree of continuity is, as expected, to be found in the use of heavy pauses, but even there the dominant trends support the traditional chronology. The graphs for Gilbert's rearrangement of *PL*, on the contrary, for the most part are inconsistent in their upward and downward movements, with no, or little, seeming continuity of development. Yet even in these graphs *PR* and *SA* show a surprising tendency to get linked with the last parts of *PL*. Even Gilbert's theories concerning the order of composition of *PL* would make us place them at the end of Milton's poetic career.

# WORD LENGTH

THE TREATMENT OF WORD LENGTH—an aspect of style seldom discussed in literary criticism except in passing—can be of decisive importance in determining the stylistic physiognomy of a writer. Not only the "sesquipedalia verba" which immediately strike the eye but also the lexical components that do not at once obtrude themselves on the reader's attention by virtue of their length demand the critic's notice if he wants to present an adequate description of an author's characteristic manner of expression, especially of his rhythm.

English is now, and was already in the Renaissance, essentially a language of monosyllables, containing also a goodly admixture of disyllabic expressions, but sparingly using words longer than that. Words whose length exceeds two syllables are customarily styled polysyllables. The present study departs from this custom, reserving this term for words of more syllables than three. Words of three syllables are here called trisyllables.

Since this is a study of verse, the number of syllables meant is always the number of metrical syllables. Elided syllables, syllables not counting in the metrical scheme, are disregarded in the statistics. "Ignominy" is normally a word of four syllables, but in Milton's line "That were an ignominy and shame beneath" (*PL* I. 115) it functions metrically as three syllables. Its final vowel, at least fictively, combines with the initial vowel of "and" into one metrical syllable. The definite article in "th' Omnipotent" (*PL* I. 49) may be a word but its vowel is elided, so for our purposes it does not count: it equals zero.

Not only the total amounts of words of different length but also their positions in the pentameter line have been taken into account, since these significantly affect the total impression. In a line like "And put to proof his high Supremacy" (*PL* I. 132), the long final word forms a weighty climax. In "Innumerable force of Spirits arm'd" (*PL* I. 101), the long initial expression forcibly dominates the line, fixing the focus of attention on its beginning. The contrast between the monosyllabic expressions in the first half-line and the long proper name occupying nearly all of the second half in "That fire the length of *Ophiucus* huge" (*PL* II. 709) determines the character of this line with its crescendo of impressiveness. In view of such differences, the statistical data here distinguish between words in three positions: words entirely confined to the first half of the pentameter ($=$ I); words placed strictly within the second half ($=$ II); and words bridging the middle point ($=$ M).

In addition to the number of words belonging in the different length categories, the statistical tables indicate also the number of syllables they occupy. Only in this way was it possible to calculate the total metrical space taken up by non-monosyllabic lexical elements.

No very extensive comparisons with the practices of other poets could be undertaken, but I have examined sample passages from the pentameters of Spenser, Marlowe, and Shakespeare. The amounts of "non-monosyllabic space" in these samples, calculated in percentages in the total number of syllables, were as follows: *The Faerie Queene*, I. i (first 200 pentameters)—40.6 per cent; *1 Tamburlaine* (first 200 pent.)—46.7; *Titus Andronicus* (first 200 pent.)—46.7; *Othello* I. iii (first 200 pent.)—39.0; *Coriolanus* I. i (173 full pent.)—40.5; *The Winter's Tale* (first 200 pent.)—32.6. The ratios show distinct stylistic divergences. The language of the passage from Spenser, carefully adorned though it be, is rather more monosyllabic than the reverberant rhetoric of Marlowe. Marlowe's polysyllabic oratory seems echoed by the young Shakespeare, whose text shows exactly the same ratio as the passage from *Tamburlaine*. In the later, less flamboyant Shakespearian passages the percentages subside.

The distribution of non-monosyllabic forms on the whole stays remarkably even throughout Milton's blank verse poetry. Nowhere in our tables does it fall below 41.4 per cent of the total syllabic space (lowest of all in *Comus*, *PL* XI, and *PR* I), and nowhere does it rise above 45.8 per cent—a maximum difference of just over 4 per cent. The average percentages for the complete works—*Comus* 42.2, *PL* 43.4, *PR* 43.3, *SA* 44.5—show a very gradual increase in the use of longer forms.

Somewhat more considerable differences in the averages for complete works become apparent as soon as we distinguish between words of different length. In the case of the disyllables—next to the monosyllables the commonest type in the language—contrasts are almost nonexistent: *Comus* 29.8, *PL* 28.6, *PR* 29.1, *SA* 28.9. There is slightly more variety in the figures for longer forms. Those for trisyllables are: *Comus* 9.7, *PL* 11.3, *PR* 11.0, *SA* 11.6; those for words longer than three syllables are: *Comus* 2.8, *PL* 3.3, *PR* 3.3, *SA* 4.1. This is an ascending scale, although the ascent is slow. The differences seem slight, but they are far from negligible. The long words, standing out as they do among the largely monosyllabic and disyllabic vocabulary, are conspicuous enough to make even minor variations in their frequency quite noticeable.

Patterns of some interest appear as we examine the more detailed information presented in the tables and graphs. As trisyllables and polysyllables become more frequent, the incidence of disyllables falls off: the commoner type of word is crowded out by the longer, more distinctive forms. Where the graphs for the longer forms—particularly the graphs combining the figures for trisyllables and polysyllables—show distinct peaks, those of disyllables have troughs, and vice versa (see Fig. XIII, Graphs 4, 5, 7, 8). In spite of the unevenness of the curves in the longer graphs an unmistakable overall pattern is apparent. Up to *PL* VIII the curve for the words longer than two syllables rises, showing only one deep intermediate drop in *PL* IV; then, after *PL* VIII, it falls off, to resume its rising movement in the second half of *PR* and in *SA*. In the shorter graphs the internal contrasts are evened out: *PL*, from Books III-IV to the end, appears as an almost faultless equilateral pyramid, culminating in Books VII-VIII. *PR* is only slightly higher than the end of *PL*; *SA* continues the upward trend begun in *PR*.

The picture is the familiar one: a movement up and away from *Comus* is followed after the middle of *PL* by a downward movement. Both *PR* and *SA* remain much closer to the later books of *PL* than to *Comus*.

The evidence convincingly illustrates an important aspect in the development of Milton's style. The language of *Comus*, rich as it is, is, for Milton, not highly polysyllabic. Polysyllables are used for ornamentation, often most conspicuously and effectively, but still, on the whole, relatively seldom. The specifically Miltonic, increasingly idiosyncratic epic manner, displaying a new kind of epic magnificence, comes into its own in *PL*, to be replaced by a barer, sparer style as the poem is moving towards its end. In *PR* the number of longer words, not great in the earlier books, increases along with the splendor of the temptations with which Satan is trying to corrupt Christ. It reaches its culmination in Book III, in the vision of the kingdoms of the world and their military glory. In *PR* III. 267-347, the passage presenting the central panorama of earthly might, the figures for non-monosyllables are exceptionally high: for all words longer than one syllable, 478 syllables per 100 lines; for trisyllables + polysyllables, 229; for polysyllables alone, 82—higher figures than any of the averages listed in our statistical tables. In *SA* the distribution of longer words is more even than in *PR*, but while the language here on the whole has that "colloquial irregularity," "massive, rugged, and sinewy," that Douglas Bush notes in it,[18] it nevertheless is liberally sprinkled with polysyllables— more so in its final section than any other part of Milton's blank verse poetry, with the sole exception of *PR* III.

Further patterns of interest are revealed by a study of the positions in the pentameter line in which the different word-length categories are placed. In *Comus* the non-monosyllabic elements of the vocabulary strongly tend towards the end of the line, whereas in *PL* the curve for the first half-line consistently stays on top, even though a very noticeable decline of it in Books IX-XII brings the two curves close together (see Fig. XIV, Graphs 1, 2). In *PR* and *SA* the overall averages for the first half-line remain much as at the end of *PL*, but those for the second half rise, making the curves diverge: a repetition of the pattern leading the situation back towards that in *Comus*, but without reaching it. The weightier verbal material, which in *Comus* heavily accentuated the latter part of the line, at first sharply recedes towards its beginning and then again slowly moves towards its end: a feature parallel to Milton's treatment of another device for emphasizing the last part of the pentameter, namely line-end pauses, the graphs for which (Fig. V, Graphs 4, 5, 7, 8) show a similar curve. Word-length arrangement and pause arrangement cooperate in making the final part of the line its climax.

The contrasts between the two half-lines, slight in the disyllables, become much more pronounced in the longer forms. They are seen most clearly in Figure XIV, Graphs 13, 14 (for trisyllables and polysyllables combined). The curve for the second half-line here moves in directions often opposed to the two other curves, the curve for the first half-line and that for the middle of the line, which in Graph 14 run approximately parallel. It is in the second half of the line that the specific intentions of the poet appear to assert themselves most strongly.

The frequencies for the different positions, viewed only in relation to each other, regardless of the number of lines (Figs. XV, XVI), provide further insights. The longer the forms in question, the sharper the ups and downs in the graphs. The crests become higher, the troughs deeper. The polysyllables, which because of their low frequencies formed rather flat curves in Figure XIV, here produce a deeply indented picture, whereas the curves for disyllables show only slight indentation, coming close to forming straight horizontal lines. The order of frequency for the different positions varies from category to category. The disyllables prefer the second half-line and conspicuously avoid the middle of the line. The trisyllables throughout *PL* predominate in the first half-line; in *PR* and *SA* they prefer the second half but the distance between the two curves dwindles considerably. The polysyllables tend strongly towards the middle of the line, the relation between the two half-lines remaining much the same as in the case of the trisyllables.

Some of these differences seem easy enough to explain: the longer the word, the more conscious manipulation is needed to accommodate it strictly within one half-line and the likelier it is to straddle the middle. This fact, however, does not account for the backward and forward trends of the different word categories. It remains to be explained why the disyllables so markedly prefer the later and not the earlier part of the pentameter. An explanation, on the face of it obvious, would be that the longer words, tending

35

towards the first half-line, crowd the disyllables out. While this may be true of *PL*, it clearly does not apply to the other poems. In *Comus*, and, less consistently and to a slighter extent, also in *PR* and *SA*, the second half predominates over the first half in all categories, not only in the disyllables.

The total picture emerging from this examination of word length in Milton's verse agrees with the traditional chronology. *PR* and *SA* maintain their position after *PL*. There are unevennesses in the internal patterns of *PL*, but none of these is considerable enough to suggest any significant chronological dislocation. The overall trends, distinctly marked, impressively coincide with the pattern observed again and again in the earlier chapters of this study: curves leading away from *Comus*, somewhere near the middle of *PL* begin to move back towards their initial level, though only seldom coming close to it. The gradual nature of the changes suggests continuity of development.

The graphs for Gilbert's chronology in the present chapter look likelier than before, but not likelier than those for the usual chronology. And as before, even an acceptance of Gilbert's views would not affect the position of *PR* and *SA*: both these works remain stubbornly linked to the end of *PL*.

# FEMININE AND PYRRHIC ENDINGS

FOR THE DETAILS concerning these two types of non-iambic line endings in Milton the reader is referred to my "Milton's Blank Verse" (pp. 160-71, 180-91). All that needs to be remarked upon here is the way the poet's use of these two types seems to fit into the picture already drawn of his stylistic development.

Feminine endings are frequent in *Comus*, become very rare in the earlier books of *PL*, but then again begin to occur more frequently, their incidence increasing considerably in *PR* and reaching a culmination in *SA*. At the same time there are changes in their phonetic nature. The heavy consonantal clusters and unvoiced consonants not uncommon in such endings in the masque are avoided in the first half of *PL*, where the extra syllables of these endings are made as inconspicuous as possible, and often capable of "fictive elision" in the sense in which Robert Bridges uses the term. The situation changes later in the poem, in *PR* and in *SA*, which show an increasing use of heavier and harsher consonantal groups.

Sonority, euphony, ease of enunciation characterize these endings in the early part of *PL*—that part of it in which Milton also in other ways strongly emphasizes ornamental dignity and splendor. Later he does not seem to make any particular efforts to avoid occasional harshness of sound, but often appears to introduce it deliberately. This is true both of the narrative passages and of the dialogue.

"Pyrrhic" endings—endings with only a light, barely felt secondary stress on the tenth metrical syllable of the line—appear frequently in *Comus*, where they often occur in clusters or are arranged to effect a quasi-stanzaic grouping of the verse. They are rare throughout *PL*, especially in its first half, but somewhat more frequent in *PR* and *SA*. In *Comus*, the words appearing in such endings, the general tone of the passages in question, and the archaic pronunciations employed to obtain the extra syllable needed for them (apparitión, self-delusión) suggest a harking back to Elizabethan times when this device was often used to achieve lyrical mellifluousness or sonorous oratorical effects. In the earlier half of *PL* clusters of final pyrrhics tend to be connected with associations of romantic glory or lyrical feeling; after *PL* VIII they are more widely scattered and their use seems more casual. Something of the early manner revives in Satan's oratory and in the descriptions of worldly luxury and might in *PR*, and, faintly, in *SA*, in the speeches of Dalila—like Satan, an agent of temptation. The early lyrical fervor connected with this device is gone, however; all that remains of its early atmosphere is some degree of oratorical emphasis. In this respect also, as in other ways, Milton is ever more noticeably turning away from an Elizabethan practice, resuming it only occasionally for special purposes.

# CONCLUSION

THROUGHOUT THE PRECEDING PAGES the main purpose of this study has been to ascertain the extent to which the evidence corroborated or contradicted the traditional notions concerning Miltonic chronology. Did the patterns that emerged seem to have meaning? Did they suggest a credible type of development? Could they be convincingly interpreted in terms of artistic and psychological evolution?

The answer to these questions was in the affirmative. Convergent evidence resulted in a picture of development which became clearer with every chapter. After largely Elizabethan beginnings Milton created his own idiosyncratic, highly individual epic style, emphatically a high style, heroic and soaring, rather consistently sustained throughout somewhat more than the first half of *PL*. Then a change set in, gradually developing and persisting, with modifications, through all the rest of Milton's poetic career. A more austere style, less orotund, less reverberant and ornamental, briefer in its rhythms, shorter in the words it used, took Milton's poetry farther and farther away from the Elizabethan, and, more specifically, the Spenserian manner which had strongly influenced his early work. The style of deliberate magnificence was now used only intermittently, when the occasion seemed to demand it, as in Satan's attempts to convert Christ to worldliness in *PR*.

Studies of mathematical progressions and regressions played an important part in these inquiries, and some surprising regularities were discovered. Even so, the human mind was not viewed as a mechanical appliance never subject to seemingly anomalous fluctuations and changes. Not all of these changes could be fully explained. The relationship between form and meaning is an area of study in which there are still vast spaces to be explored.

My main criticism of my principal critic, Mr. John T. Shawcross, is precisely that he has made too few attempts to examine that relationship—that he relies too exclusively on mere statistics, that is, arithmetic. Taking the figures I had presented in "Milton's Blank Verse," he rearranged them in descending and ascending order and drew his conclusions from the results. That a line of development need not constantly move in just one direction did not seem to have occurred to him.

CONCLUSION

Having made some extensive inquiries in connection with my study of Renaissance pause patterns, I believe I am in a position to suggest what might happen to Shakespearian chronology if such an almost completely unadulterated mathematical method were applied. Let us consider one of the features examined in the present monograph, the relation of pauses in the first half to those in the second half of the pentameter line. The figures for *King Lear*, according to the First Folio, are: Act I—89 : 182 (32.8 : 67.2), Act II—150 : 222 (40.3 : 59.7), Act III—91 : 140 (39.4 : 60.6), Act IV—154 : 232 (39.9 : 60.1), Act V—121 : 165 (42.2 : 57.8); for the play as a whole—605 : 944 (39.1 : 60.9). Since the tendency in Shakespeare is towards an increasing use of pauses in the second half-line, strict mathematics would have to suggest the following order of composition: V, II, IV, III, I. The first part would have to come last, the last first—approximately as in the redating of the parts of *PL*. In the case of *Macbeth* a somewhat more credible situation would arise. The figures for the acts of that play are: I—106 : 182 (36.8 : 63.2), II—85 : 151 (36.0 : 64.0), III—119 : 181 (39.7 : 60.3), IV—109 : 212 (34.0 : 66.0), V—58 : 149 (28.0 : 72.0). The third act would come first whereas the rest of the play would not be affected. But chronological disintegrationism could go further than this. It might also be considered whether some of the acts may not have been written much earlier or later than the main body of the plays. Act V of *Macbeth*, for example, could be held to have been written several years later, between *Antony and Cleopatra* (ratio 29.6 : 70.4) and *Coriolanus* (29.8 : 70.2), or after *The Tempest* (33.6 : 66.4), just before *Henry VIII* (ratio for parts generally accepted as Shakespearian 25.2 : 74.8). If no other information were available to prevent such speculations, we might soon come across them in scholarly papers.

Shawcross' approach is of course more sophisticated than this. He examines not just one prosodical phenomenon but a number of them. Nevertheless, he seldom attempts to relate form to meaning. Besides, he considers almost exclusively those aspects of verse that were discussed in my earlier paper, without broadening the field.

The present study does broaden the field considerably. Instead of only the strong punctuation, all of Milton's punctuation has been examined. Instead of confining myself to polysyllables, I have tried to cover the entire problem of word length. The -ed participles and adjectives, the *compleat steel* type of phrase have been reexamined in much larger contexts. Everything has been compared with the parallel data resulting from Gilbert's rearrangement of *PL*. The results, it seems to me, admit of no doubt: the old chronology in its main outlines seems unassailable. Some questions may still arise, for instance, concerning the relative positions of *PR* and *SA*. Both clearly belong in Milton's last period, but which came first? It might be tempting to place *PR* later. *SA* would then appear as the last great emotional outburst of Milton, whereas *PR* would have been written after the inward tempests had blown over, with "calm of mind, all passion spent."

It seems to me, however, that here we have reached the point where confident conclusions become impossible. The same is true of many problems in the internal chronology of *PL*. Passages may have been shifted, inserted, revised—that much it would be most unreasonable not to admit. But, as far as I can see, we have no means of determining exactly where and when. We have to recognize the limits set to our methods of inquiry.

This may be the right place for a few remarks about Shawcross' redating of *PR*. He has made his conclusions so completely dependent on the theories of Parker and Gilbert that without their support his intricate edifice must collapse. If the main conclusions arrived at in this monograph are correct, then his contentions must be found to be invalid. *PR*, which he quite rightly links with *SA*, has, in the light of the evidence presented in the present paper, exactly because of its links with the tragedy, even if no other reasons did exist, to be regarded as late. I have shown many other reasons as well.

There is, nevertheless, at least one feature in Shawcross' observations that seems fruitful. He has called attention to some aspects of the prosody of *PR*—above all, the way feminine endings are used—that show the influence of dramatic verse on the dialogue in the poem. These peculiarities do not conflict with the total style of the work and they do not seem to me to permit any chronological conclusions, but they are of interest. The analysis would have been even more interesting if Shawcross had noticed what Louis L. Martz describes as the "contest of styles" in the epic: the use of the "middle style" in the earlier parts, the oratorical "high style" of Satan, the simpler language of Christ.[19] The way in which these contrasts, which doubtless were used deliberately, may be reflected in the prosody would be a fascinating subject to explore. Some of these contrasts have been pointed out in the preceding pages. Several of them are sharp, but, surprisingly, they do not affect the statistical averages for the work as a whole in a way that would make it seem out of place in the position it occupies close before the end of our graphs. A feeling for total configuration, for "Gestalt," seems to have dominated the changes and contrasts in this poem, as apparently it does throughout the wide range of Milton's poetry.

## NOTES

1. Cambridge, Mass., p. 441.
2. *The Composition of Paradise Lost* (Chapel Hill, 1947), p. 14n.
3. See John S. Diekhoff, "Rime in Paradise Lost" (*PMLA*, XLI, 539-43); A. Oras, "Echoing Verse Endings in Paradise Lost" (*South Atlantic Studies for Sturgis E. Leavitt*, Washington, 1953), pp. 175-90.
4. *Op. cit.*, p. 164.
5. For another, much harsher criticism of the views of Parker and Gilbert concerning the date of *Samson*, see Ernest Sirluck, "Milton's Idle Right Hand," Appendix (*Journal of English and Germanic Philology*, LX, 1961), pp. 773-81.
6. *John Milton* (New York, 1964), p. 194.
7. For list of passages composing these groups see Appendix.
8. *Op. cit.*, p. 142.
9. *SAMLA Studies in Milton* (Gainesville, Fla., 1953), pp. 128-97.
10. Shawcross, *op. cit.*, pp. 348-49.
11. Robert Bridges, *Milton's Prosody* (Oxford, 1921), p. 73.
12. F. T. Prince, *The Italian Element in Milton's Verse* (Oxford, 1953). See also A. Oras, "Milton's 'Upon the Circumcision' and Tasso" (*Notes and Queries*, Vol. 197, pp. 314-15) and "Milton's Early Rhyme Schemes and the Structure of *Lycidas*" (*Modern Philology*, LII, 12-22).
13. This becomes particularly apparent in the adjective + noun + adjective pattern so favored by Milton. Compare such early instances as: the dark foundations deep (*Nat. Ode* 123), flicking shadows pale (*ibid.* 232), winged Warriors bright (*Circumcision* 1), unbleproved pleasures free (*L'Allegro* 40), unblest inchanter vile (*Comus* 907) with the following later examples: eternal Warr Irreconcileable (*PL* I. 121-22), the blessed Spirits elect (*PL* III. 310), Of conjugal attraction unreprov'd (*PL* IV. 493), jealous leer maligne (*PL* IV. 503), a horrid rift abortive (*PR* IV. 411), redundant locks/ Robustious (*SA* 568-69). In the early verse the short adjective, often following longer forms, tends to add a touch of intimacy to what might otherwise have been a too obviously literary, learned phrase not fitting very well into the gentler, warmer tone of these poems. In the later verse, the long forms seem intended to prevent precisely this impression of intimate homeliness; they raise such phrases to the level of Milton's high style, deliberately aloof in its sublimity.

14. Shawcross, *op. cit.*, p. 346.
15. See John S. Diekhoff, "The Trinity Manuscript and the Dictation of PARADISE LOST" (*Philological Quarterly*, XXVIII, 47) on the manuscript of *Comus:* "The Trinity Manuscript draft is a final draft, the basis for clean copy for publication or performance, but it is not itself clean copy." Even this may be saying too much, unless Milton himself was to produce the clean copy: not everything in the MS is likely to have been easily decipherable by a scribe.
16. The 1645 text of *Comus*, the first edition of *PL*, and the original edition of *PR* and *SA*, according to Harris Fletcher's facsimile reproductions (Urbana, 1943).
17. See pp. 35-41.
18. *Op. cit.*, p. 194.
19. Louis L. Martz, *The Paradise Within* (New Haven, 1964), pp. 183 ff.

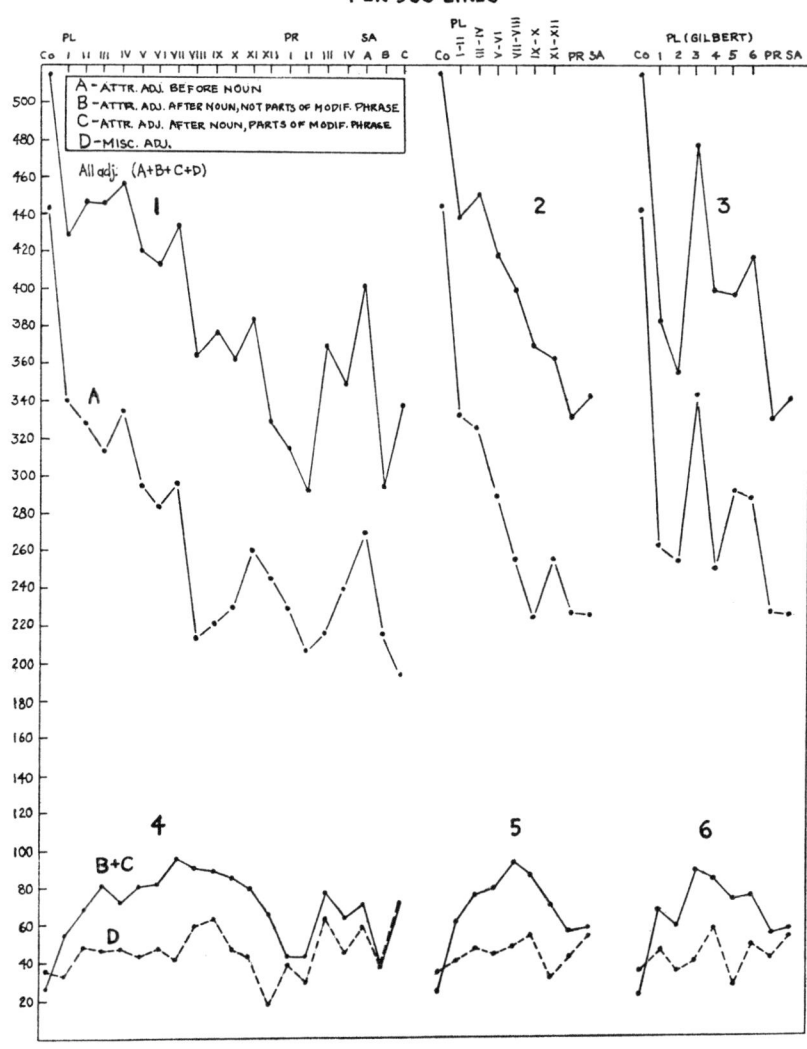

I. ADJECTIVES AND ADJECTIVAL PARTICIPLES PER 500 LINES

43

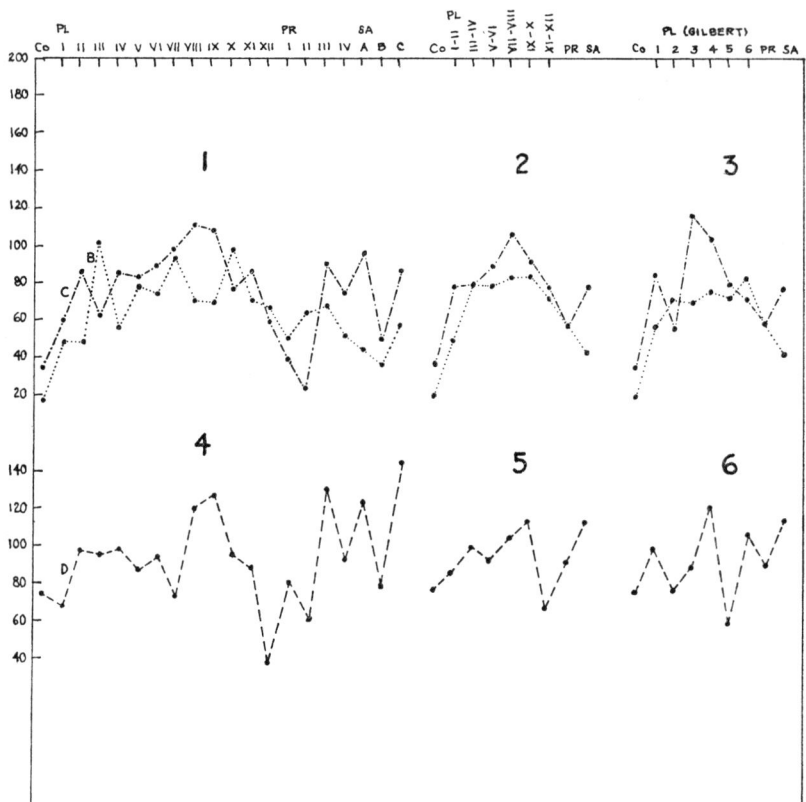

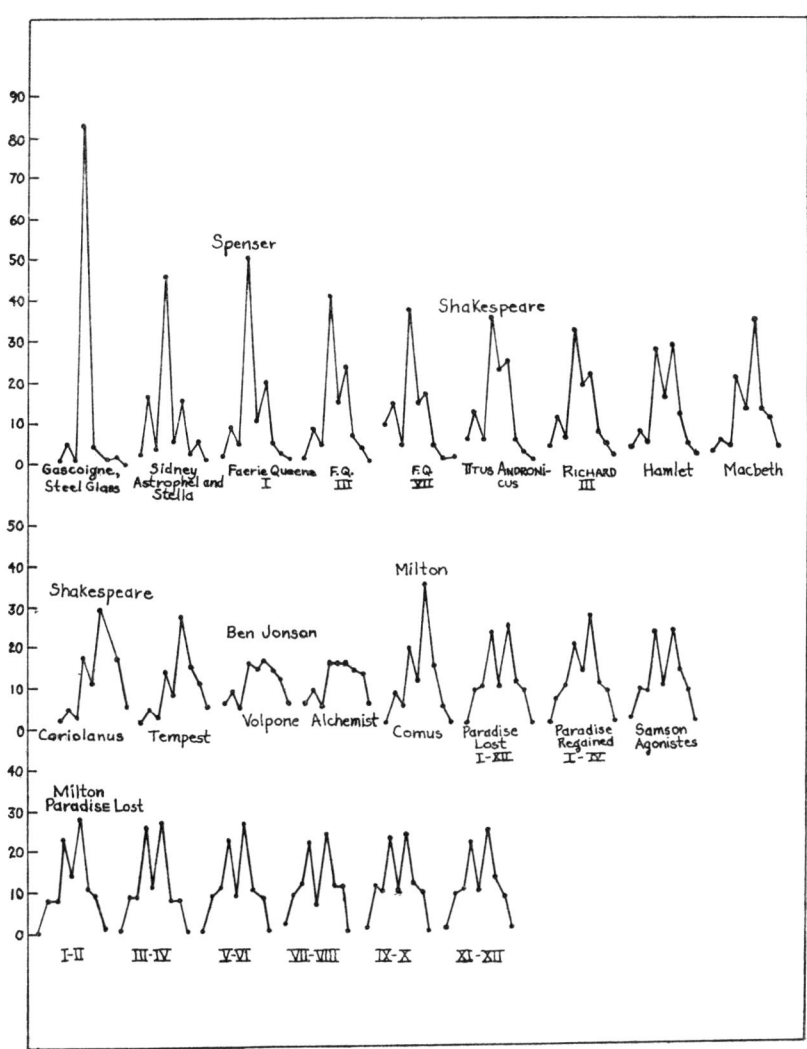

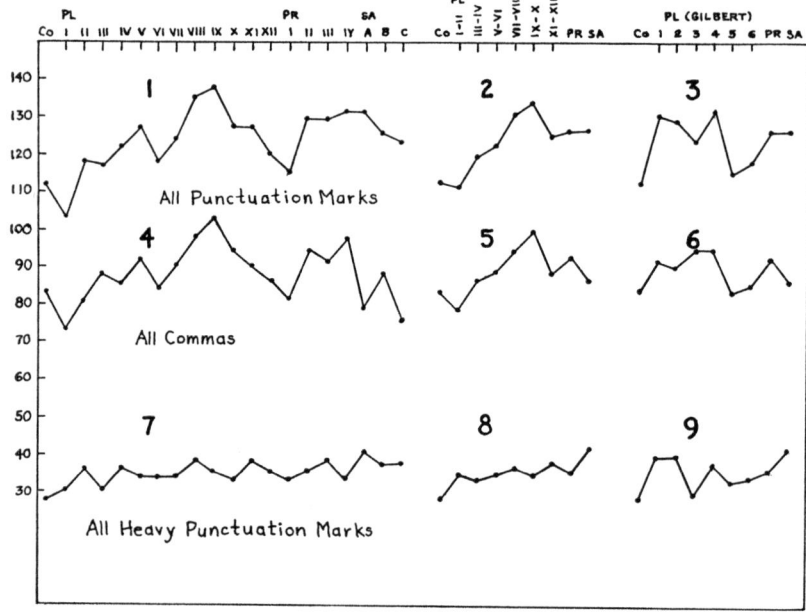

V

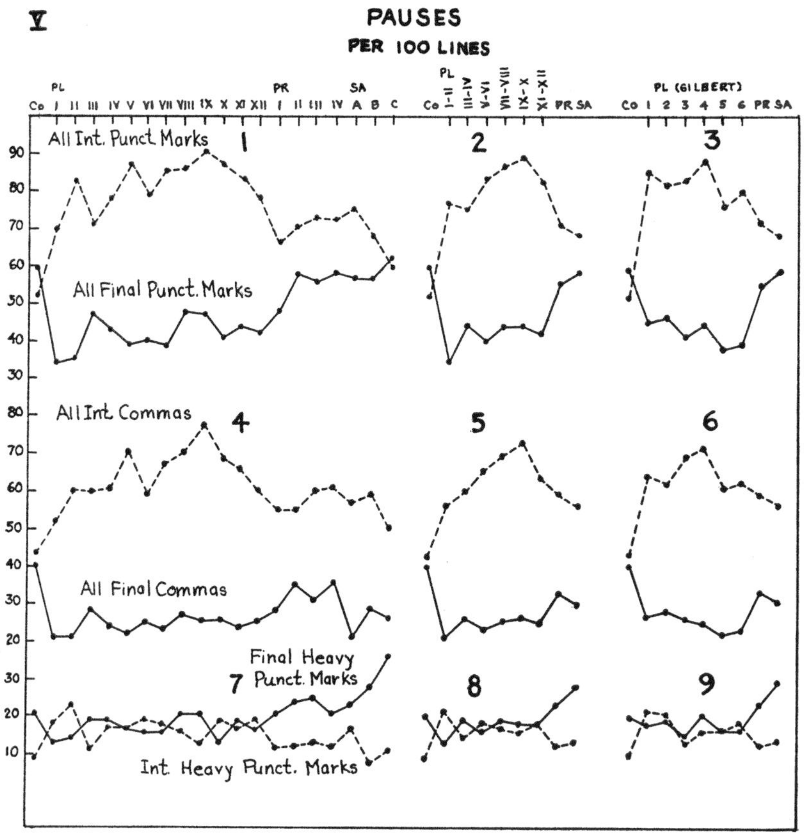
PAUSES
PER 100 LINES
PL
Co I II III IV V VI VII VIII IX X XI XII
PR
I II III IV
SA
A B C
PL
Co I-II III-IV V-VI VII-VIII IX-X XI-XII PR SA
PL (GILBERT)
Co 1 2 3 4 5 6 PR SA
All Int. Punct. Marks
All Final Punct. Marks
All Int. Commas
All Final Commas
Final Heavy Punct. Marks
Int. Heavy Punct. Marks
1
2
3
4
5
6
7
8
9
90
80
70
60
50
40
30
20
10

## VI. PAUSES
Ratios of Final to Internal Punctuation Marks
(Percentages Regardless of Number of Lines)

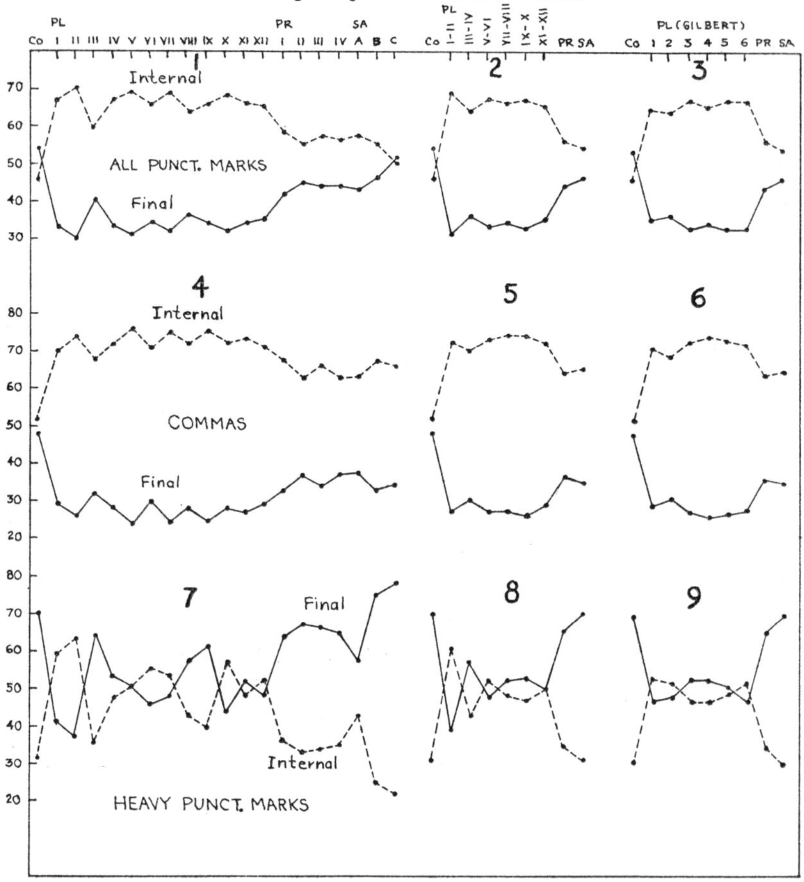

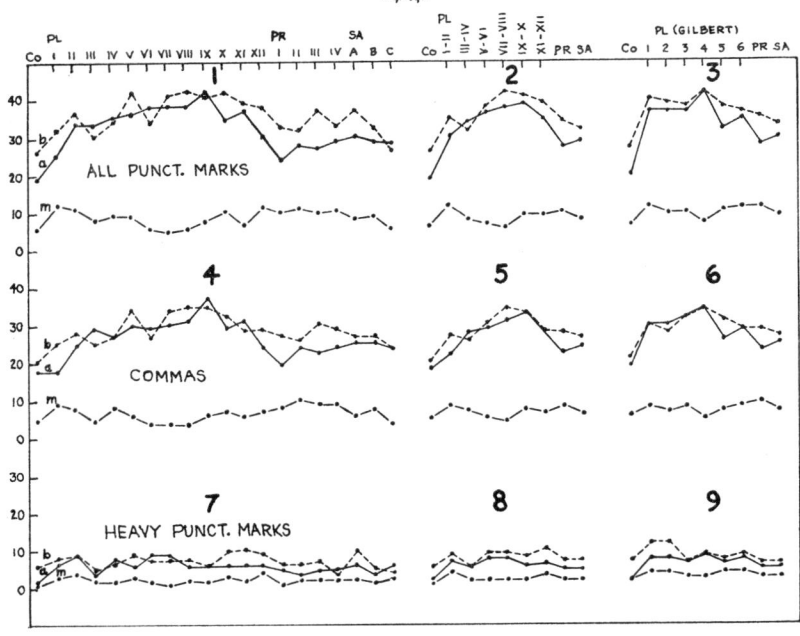

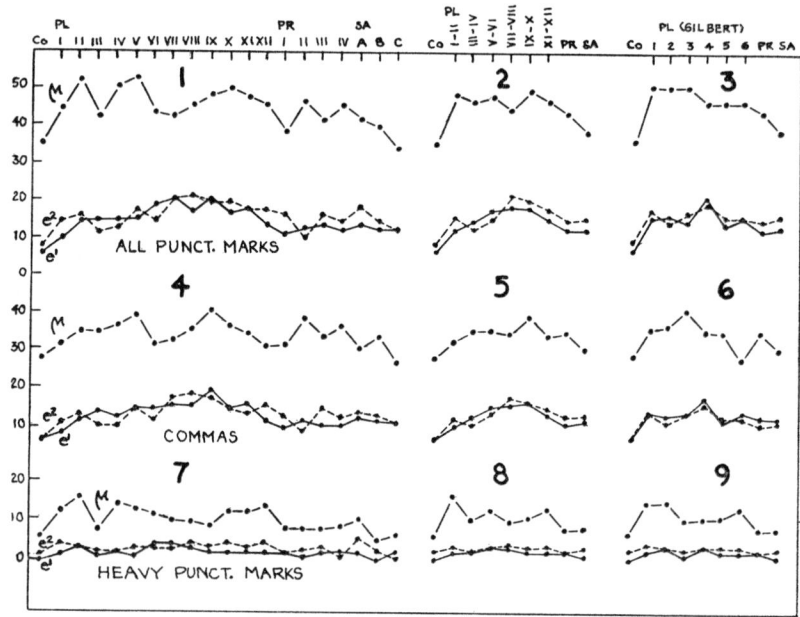

VIII PAUSES PER 100 LINES
$e^1, M, e^2$

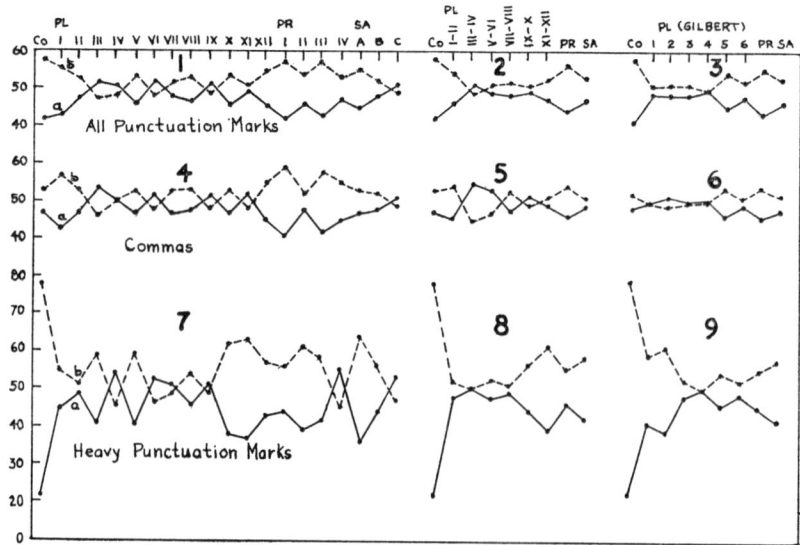

IX PAUSES IN FIRST HALF AND SECOND HALF OF LINE
Ratios of a to b (a+b=100)

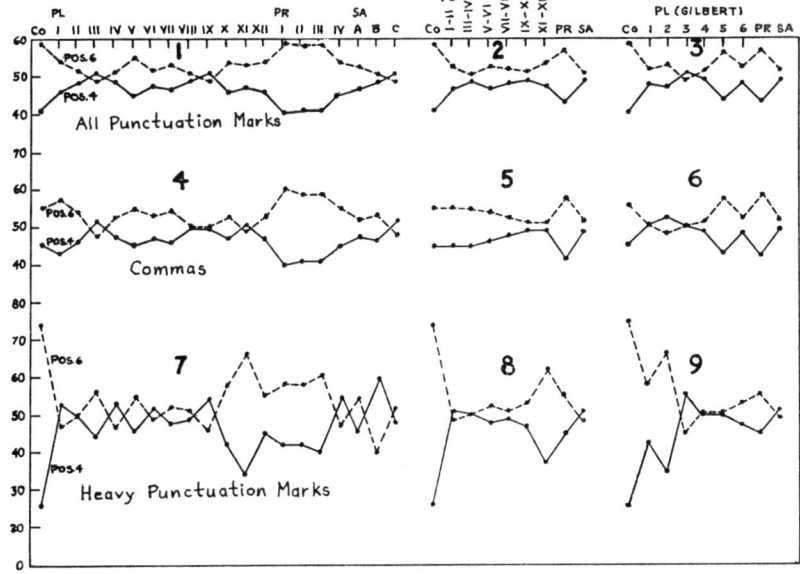

X PAUSES
Ratios of Position 4 to Position 6 (Pos.4 + Pos.6 = 100)

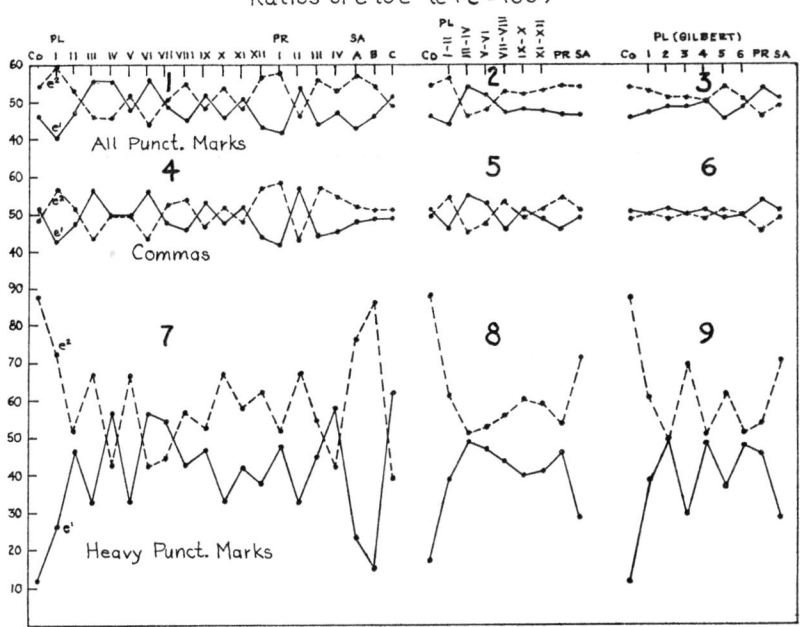

XI EXTREME PAUSES
Ratios of $e^1$ to $e^2$ ($e^1 + e^2 = 100$)

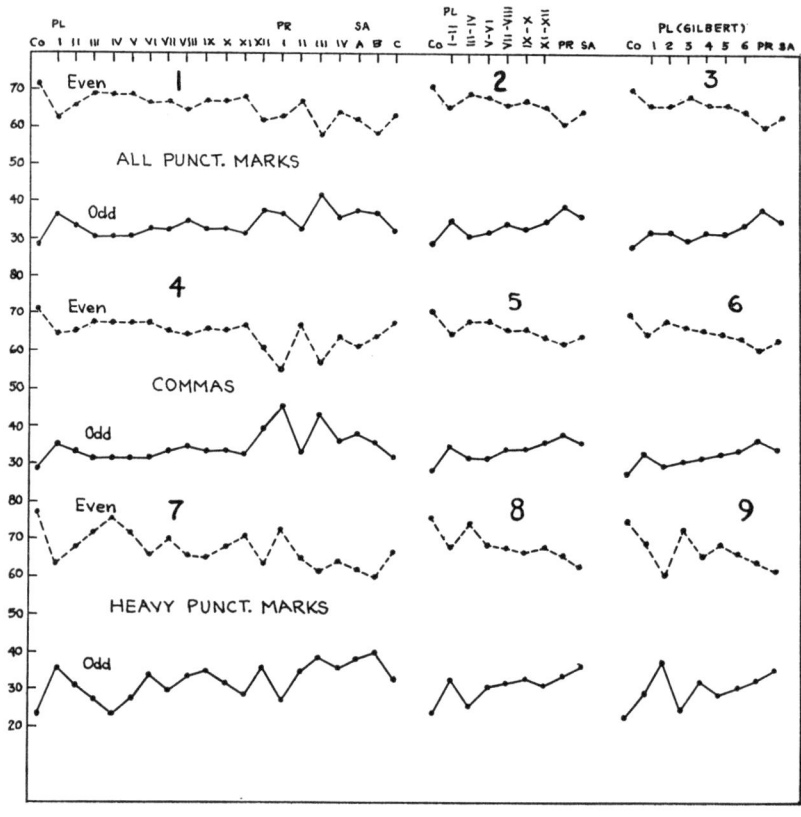

# XIII WORD LENGTH
Number of Syllables Per 100 Lines

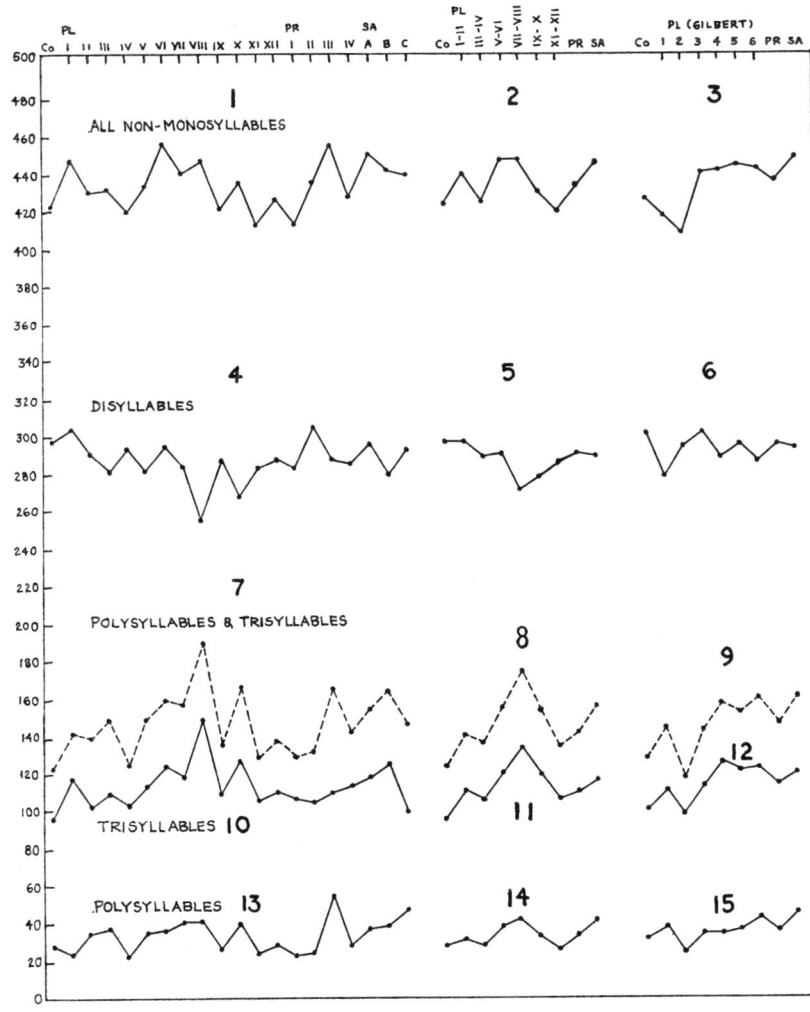

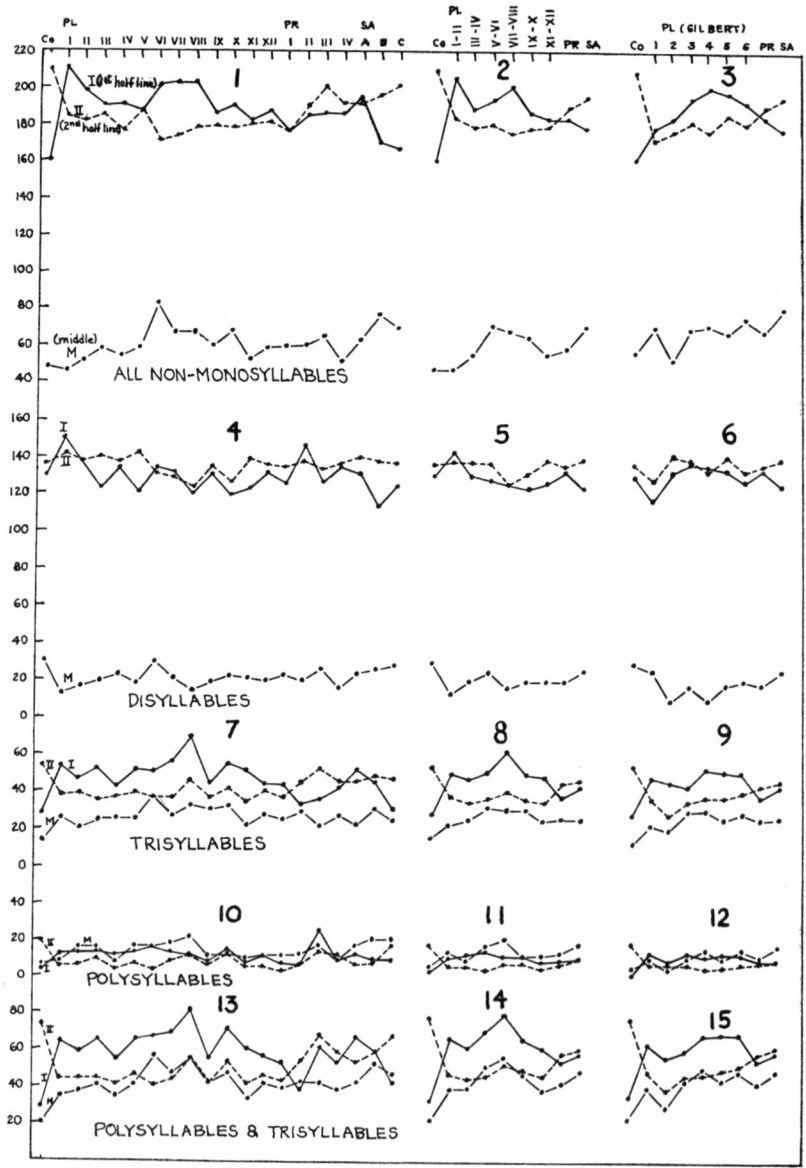

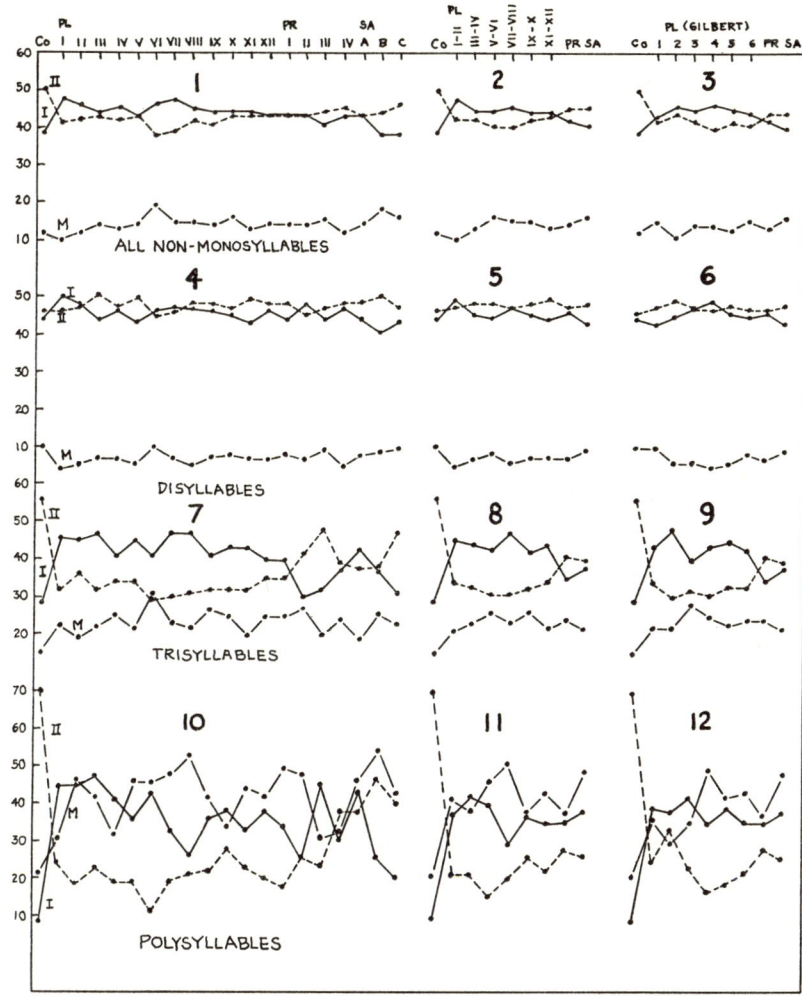

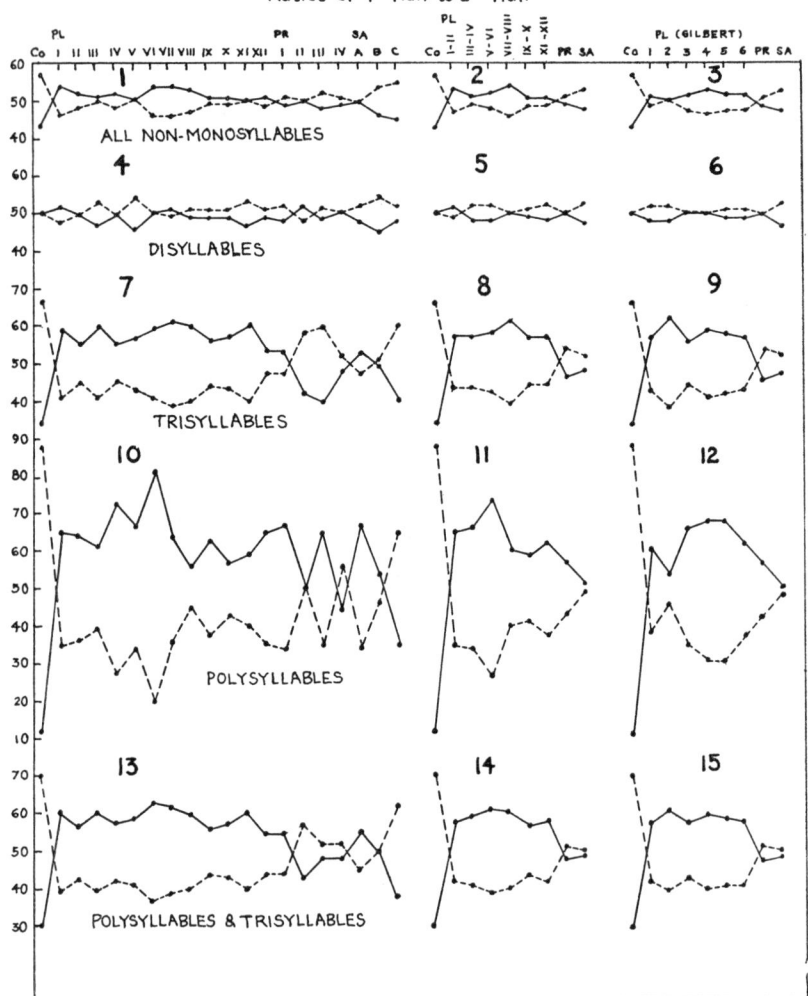

XVI WORD LENGTH
Ratios of 1st Half to 2nd Half

## I. ADJECTIVES AND ADJECTIVAL PARTICIPLES

| | No. of Lines | Absolute Figures | | | | | | | Per 100 Lines | | | | | | | |
|---|---|---|---|---|---|---|---|---|---|---|---|---|---|---|---|---|
| | | A | B | C | B+C | A+B+C | D | All Ad. & Ad.P. | A | B | C | B+C | A+B+C | D | All Ad. & Ad.P. | A : B : C : D (Totals = 100.0) |
| *Comus* | 792 | 701 | 15 | 27 | 42 | 743 | 58 | 801 | 88.5 | 1.9 | 3.4 | 5.3 | 93.8 | 7.5 | 101.1 | 87.5 : 1.9 : 3.4 : 7.2 |
| *PL* I | 798 | 542 | 39 | 49 | 88 | 630 | 55 | 685 | 67.9 | 4.9 | 6.0 | 10.9 | 78.8 | 6.9 | 85.7 | 79.1 : 5.7 : 7.2 : 8.0 |
| II | 1055 | 693 | 53 | 92 | 145 | 838 | 102 | 940 | 65.7 | 5.0 | 8.7 | 13.7 | 79.4 | 9.7 | 89.1 | 73.7 : 5.6 : 9.8 : 10.9 |
| III | 742 | 467 | 75 | 47 | 122 | 589 | 72 | 661 | 62.9 | 10.1 | 6.3 | 16.4 | 79.4 | 9.6 | 89.1 | 70.7 : 11.3 : 7.1 : 10.9 |
| IV | 1015 | 681 | 58 | 88 | 146 | 827 | 99 | 926 | 67.1 | 5.7 | 8.7 | 14.4 | 81.5 | 9.8 | 91.2 | 73.5 : 6.3 : 9.5 : 10.7 |
| V | 904 | 535 | 71 | 76 | 147 | 682 | 80 | 762 | 59.0 | 7.8 | 8.4 | 16.2 | 75.2 | 8.8 | 84.0 | 70.2 : 9.3 : 10.0 : 10.5 |
| VI | 912 | 517 | 68 | 82 | 150 | 667 | 87 | 754 | 56.7 | 7.5 | 9.0 | 16.4 | 73.2 | 9.5 | 82.7 | 68.6 : 9.0 : 10.9 : 11.5 |
| VII | 640 | 378 | 60 | 63 | 123 | 501 | 53 | 554 | 59.1 | 9.4 | 9.8 | 19.2 | 78.3 | 8.3 | 86.6 | 68.2 : 10.8 : 11.4 : 9.6 |
| VIII | 649 | 278 | 46 | 72 | 118 | 396 | 78 | 474 | 42.8 | 7.1 | 11.1 | 18.2 | 61.0 | 12.0 | 73.0 | 58.6 : 9.7 : 15.2 : 16.5 |
| IX | 1189 | 528 | 83 | 130 | 213 | 741 | 152 | 893 | 44.1 | 7.0 | 10.9 | 17.9 | 62.3 | 12.7 | 75.1 | 59.1 : 9.3 : 14.6 : 17.0 |
| X | 1104 | 510 | 108 | 79 | 187 | 697 | 105 | 802 | 46.2 | 9.8 | 7.7 | 16.9 | 63.1 | 9.5 | 72.6 | 63.6 : 13.5 : 9.8 : 13.1 |
| XI | 897 | 469 | 65 | 78 | 143 | 612 | 79 | 691 | 52.0 | 7.2 | 8.6 | 15.9 | 67.9 | 8.8 | 76.7 | 67.9 : 9.4 : 11.3 : 11.4 |
| XII | 644 | 319 | 43 | 39 | 82 | 401 | 25 | 426 | 49.2 | 6.6 | 6.0 | 12.6 | 61.8 | 3.8 | 65.6 | 74.9 : 10.1 : 9.1 : 5.8 |
| | 10549 | 5917 | 769 | 895 | 1664 | 7581 | 987 | 8568 | 56.1 | 7.3 | 8.5 | 15.8 | 71.9 | 9.3 | 81.2 | 69.1 : 9.0 : 10.4 : 11.5 |
| *PR* I | 502 | 231 | 25 | 19 | 44 | 275 | 40 | 315 | 46.0 | 5.0 | 3.8 | 8.8 | 54.8 | 8.0 | 62.7 | 73.3 : 7.9 : 6.0 : 12.7 |
| II | 486 | 211 | 31 | 12 | 43 | 254 | 30 | 284 | 43.4 | 6.4 | 2.4 | 8.8 | 52.3 | 6.2 | 58.4 | 74.3 : 10.9 : 4.2 : 10.6 |
| III | 443 | 200 | 30 | 40 | 70 | 270 | 57 | 327 | 45.1 | 6.8 | 9.0 | 15.8 | 60.9 | 12.9 | 73.8 | 61.2 : 9.2 : 12.2 : 17.4 |
| IV | 639 | 306 | 33 | 48 | 81 | 387 | 59 | 446 | 47.9 | 5.2 | 7.5 | 12.7 | 60.6 | 9.2 | 69.8 | 68.6 : 7.4 : 10.8 : 13.2 |
| | 2070 | 948 | 119 | 119 | 238 | 1186 | 186 | 1372 | 45.8 | 5.75 | 5.75 | 11.5 | 57.3 | 9.0 | 66.3 | 69.1 : 8.7 : 8.7 : 13.5 |
| *SA* (A) | 474 | 255 | 21 | 46 | 67 | 322 | 58 | 380 | 53.8 | 4.4 | 9.7 | 14.1 | 67.9 | 12.2 | 80.2 | 67.1 : 5.5 : 12.1 : 15.3 |
| (B) | 492 | 211 | 13 | 25 | 38 | 249 | 39 | 288 | 42.9 | 2.6 | 5.1 | 7.7 | 50.6 | 7.9 | 58.5 | 73.3 : 4.5 : 8.7 : 13.5 |
| (C) | 372 | 144 | 22 | 32 | 54 | 198 | 53 | 251 | 38.7 | 5.9 | 8.6 | 14.5 | 53.2 | 14.3 | 67.5 | 57.4 : 8.8 : 12.7 : 21.1 |
| | 1338 | 610 | 56 | 103 | 159 | 769 | 150 | 919 | 45.6 | 4.2 | 7.7 | 11.9 | 57.5 | 11.2 | 68.7 | 66.3 : 6.1 : 11.2 : 16.4 |

I. ADJECTIVES AND ADJECTIVAL PARTICIPLES (*Continued*)

| | No. of Lines | Absolute Figures | | | | | | Per 100 Lines | | | | | | | A : B : C : D (Totals = 100.0) |
|---|---|---|---|---|---|---|---|---|---|---|---|---|---|---|---|
| | | A | B | C | B+C | A+B+C | D | All Ad. & Ad. P. | A | B | C | B+C | A+B+C | D | All Ad. & Ad. P. | |
| *PL* I-II | 1853 | 1235 | 92 | 141 | 233 | 1468 | 157 | 1625 | 66.6 | 5.0 | 7.6 | 12.6 | 79.2 | 8.5 | 87.7 | 76.0 : 5.7 : 8.7 : 9.7 |
| III-IV | 1767 | 1148 | 133 | 135 | 268 | 1416 | 171 | 1587 | 65.3 | 7.6 | 7.7 | 15.3 | 80.6 | 9.7 | 90.3 | 72.3 : 8.4 : 8.5 : 10.8 |
| V-VI | 1816 | 1052 | 139 | 158 | 297 | 1349 | 167 | 1516 | 57.9 | 7.7 | 8.7 | 16.4 | 74.3 | 9.2 | 83.5 | 69.4 : 9.2 : 10.4 : 11.0 |
| VII-VIII | 1289 | 656 | 106 | 135 | 241 | 897 | 131 | 1028 | 51.0 | 8.2 | 10.5 | 18.7 | 69.6 | 10.2 | 79.7 | 63.8 : 10.3 : 13.1 : 12.7 |
| IX-X | 2293 | 1038 | 191 | 209 | 400 | 1438 | 257 | 1695 | 45.3 | 8.3 | 9.1 | 17.4 | 62.7 | 11.2 | 73.9 | 61.2 : 11.3 : 12.3 : 15.2 |
| XI-XII | 1541 | 788 | 108 | 117 | 225 | 1013 | 104 | 1117 | 51.1 | 7.0 | 7.6 | 14.6 | 65.7 | 6.7 | 72.5 | 70.5 : 9.7 : 10.5 : 9.3 |
| | 10549 | 5917 | 769 | 895 | 1664 | 7581 | 987 | 8568 | 56.1 | 7.3 | 8.5 | 15.8 | 71.9 | 9.3 | 81.2 | 66.3 : 6.1 : 11.2 : 16.4 |
| *PL* (Gilbert) | | | | | | | | | | | | | | | | |
| I | 1549 | 821 | 86 | 129 | 215 | 1036 | 152 | 1188 | 53.0 | 5.6 | 8.3 | 13.9 | 66.9 | 9.8 | 76.7 | 69.1 : 7.2 : 10.9 : 12.8 |
| II | 491 | 251 | 35 | 27 | 62 | 313 | 37 | 350 | 51.1 | 7.1 | 5.5 | 12.6 | 63.7 | 7.5 | 71.3 | 71.7 : 10.0 : 7.7 : 10.6 |
| III | 817 | 560 | 57 | 94 | 151 | 711 | 71 | 782 | 68.5 | 6.9 | 11.5 | 18.4 | 86.9 | 8.8 | 95.7 | 71.6 : 7.3 : 12.0 : 9.1 |
| IV | 2439 | 1227 | 184 | 249 | 433 | 1660 | 291 | 1951 | 50.3 | 7.6 | 10.2 | 17.8 | 68.1 | 11.9 | 80.0 | 62.8 : 9.4 : 12.8 : 14.9 |
| V | 2499 | 1464 | 180 | 197 | 377 | 1841 | 149 | 1990 | 58.6 | 7.2 | 7.9 | 15.1 | 73.7 | 5.9 | 79.6 | 73.5 : 9.0 : 9.9 : 7.5 |
| VI | 2769 | 1594 | 227 | 199 | 426 | 2020 | 287 | 2307 | 57.6 | 8.2 | 7.2 | 15.4 | 73.0 | 10.3 | 83.4 | 69.1 : 9.8 : 8.6 : 12.4 |
| | 10564* | 5917 | 769 | 895 | 1664 | 7581 | 987 | 8568 | 56.1 | 7.3 | 8.5 | 15.8 | 71.9 | 9.3 | 81.2 | 66.3 : 6.1 : 11.2 : 16.4 |

* Gilbert has not excluded in his counts the few lines added in the 2nd edition of *PL*. The difference, however, is too slight to affect the percentages.

## II. PAUSES—ALL PUNCTUATION MARKS

| | ABSOLUTE FIGURES | | | | | | | | | | INTERNAL | | | | | | | | | | FINAL | | INT. & FINAL | |
|---|---|---|---|---|---|---|---|---|---|---|---|---|---|---|---|---|---|---|---|---|---|---|---|---|
| | 1 | 2 | 3 | 4 | 5 | 6 | 7 | 8 | 9 | Total | Per 100 Lines | \multicolumn{9}{c}{PAUSES IN REL. TO EACH OTHER} | | All | Per 100 Lines | All | Per 100 Lines |
| | | | | | | | | | | | | 1 | 2 | 3 | 4 | 5 | 6 | 7 | 8 | 9 | | | | |
| Comus | 3 | 34 | 20 | 97 | 45 | 141 | 43 | 21 | 4 | 408 | 51.5 | 0.7 | 8.3 | 4.9 | 23.8 | 11.0 | 34.6 | 10.5 | 5.1 | 1.0 | 469 | 59.2 | 877 | 110.7 |
| PL I | 3 | 39 | 36 | 121 | 96 | 142 | 67 | 45 | 6 | 555 | 69.5 | 0.5 | 7.0 | 6.5 | 21.8 | 17.3 | 25.6 | 12.1 | 8.1 | 1.1 | 268 | 33.8 | 823 | 103.1 |
| II | 5 | 72 | 76 | 204 | 119 | 225 | 82 | 78 | 10 | 871 | 82.6 | 0.6 | 8.3 | 8.7 | 23.4 | 13.7 | 25.8 | 9.4 | 8.7 | 1.3 | 369 | 35.0 | 1240 | 117.5 |
| III | 8 | 52 | 50 | 134 | 57 | 130 | 40 | 44 | 8 | 523 | 70.5 | 1.5 | 9.9 | 9.6 | 25.6 | 10.9 | 24.9 | 7.7 | 8.4 | 1.5 | 347 | 46.8 | 870 | 117.3 |
| IV | 8 | 70 | 74 | 206 | 91 | 219 | 64 | 57 | 6 | 795 | 78.3 | 1.0 | 8.8 | 9.3 | 25.9 | 11.5 | 27.5 | 8.1 | 7.2 | 0.7 | 439 | 43.3 | 1234 | 121.6 |
| V | 11 | 62 | 74 | 181 | 80 | 220 | 74 | 78 | 9 | 789 | 87.2 | 1.4 | 7.8 | 9.4 | 25.2 | 10.1 | 27.9 | 9.4 | 9.9 | 1.1 | 356 | 39.4 | 1145 | 126.6 |
| VI | 7 | 71 | 97 | 167 | 53 | 179 | 68 | 61 | 7 | 710 | 77.9 | 1.0 | 10.0 | 13.6 | 23.5 | 7.4 | 25.2 | 9.6 | 8.6 | 1.0 | 368 | 40.4 | 1078 | 118.3 |
| VII | 7 | 56 | 68 | 114 | 34 | 130 | 60 | 65 | 12 | 546 | 85.3 | 1.3 | 10.3 | 12.4 | 20.9 | 6.2 | 23.8 | 11.0 | 11.9 | 2.2 | 249 | 38.9 | 795 | 124.2 |
| VIII | 9 | 43 | 66 | 128 | 41 | 131 | 74 | 65 | 4 | 561 | 86.4 | 1.6 | 7.7 | 11.7 | 22.8 | 7.3 | 23.4 | 13.2 | 11.6 | 0.7 | 313 | 48.2 | 874 | 134.7 |
| IX | 12 | 118 | 121 | 252 | 90 | 244 | 134 | 103 | 3 | 1077 | 90.6 | 1.1 | 11.0 | 11.2 | 23.4 | 8.4 | 22.6 | 12.4 | 9.6 | 0.3 | 558 | 46.9 | 1635 | 137.5 |
| X | 7 | 95 | 85 | 204 | 105 | 240 | 117 | 99 | 5 | 957 | 86.7 | 0.7 | 9.9 | 8.9 | 21.3 | 11.0 | 25.1 | 12.2 | 10.3 | 0.5 | 448 | 40.6 | 1405 | 127.3 |
| XI | 7 | 81 | 75 | 170 | 66 | 194 | 90 | 63 | 6 | 752 | 83.8 | 0.9 | 10.8 | 10.0 | 22.6 | 8.8 | 25.7 | 12.0 | 8.4 | 0.8 | 392 | 43.7 | 1144 | 127.4 |
| XII | 4 | 37 | 47 | 106 | 68 | 124 | 72 | 44 | 2 | 504 | 78.3 | 0.8 | 7.4 | 9.3 | 20.1 | 13.5 | 24.6 | 14.3 | 8.7 | 0.4 | 269 | 41.8 | 773 | 120.0 |
| | 88 | 796 | 869 | 1987 | 900 | 2178 | 942 | 802 | 78 | 8640 | 81.8 | 1.0 | 9.2 | 10.1 | 23.0 | 10.4 | 25.2 | 10.9 | 9.3 | 0.9 | 4376 | 41.5 | 13016 | 123.4 |
| PR I | 2 | 26 | 31 | 60 | 48 | 88 | 38 | 35 | 5 | 333 | 66.3 | 0.6 | 7.8 | 9.3 | 18.0 | 14.4 | 26.4 | 11.4 | 10.5 | 1.5 | 242 | 48.2 | 575 | 114.5 |
| II | 2 | 28 | 32 | 72 | 53 | 102 | 27 | 27 | 1 | 344 | 70.8 | 0.5 | 8.1 | 9.4 | 20.9 | 15.4 | 29.7 | 7.8 | 7.8 | 0.3 | 284 | 58.4 | 628 | 129.2 |
| III | 2 | 14 | 44 | 58 | 43 | 85 | 48 | 29 | — | 323 | 72.9 | 0.6 | 4.3 | 13.6 | 18.0 | 13.3 | 26.3 | 14.9 | 9.0 | — | 249 | 56.2 | 572 | 129.1 |
| IV | 4 | 31 | 46 | 107 | 61 | 123 | 52 | 35 | 6 | 465 | 72.8 | 0.8 | 6.7 | 9.9 | 23.0 | 13.1 | 26.5 | 11.2 | 7.5 | 1.3 | 369 | 57.7 | 834 | 130.5 |
| | 10 | 99 | 153 | 297 | 205 | 398 | 165 | 126 | 12 | 1465 | 70.8 | 0.7 | 6.8 | 10.4 | 20.2 | 14.0 | 27.2 | 11.3 | 8.6 | 0.8 | 1144 | 55.3 | 2609 | 126.0 |
| SA (A) | 5 | 33 | 29 | 75 | 39 | 83 | 57 | 29 | 4 | 354 | 74.7 | 1.4 | 9.3 | 8.2 | 21.2 | 11.0 | 23.4 | 16.1 | 8.2 | 1.1 | 268 | 56.5 | 622 | 131.2 |
| (B) | 6 | 27 | 30 | 77 | 41 | 80 | 43 | 28 | 4 | 336 | 68.3 | 1.8 | 8.0 | 8.9 | 22.9 | 12.2 | 23.8 | 12.8 | 8.3 | 1.2 | 278 | 56.5 | 614 | 124.8 |
| (C) | 5 | 23 | 21 | 55 | 20 | 53 | 24 | 21 | 2 | 224 | 60.2 | 2.2 | 10.3 | 9.4 | 24.5 | 8.9 | 23.7 | 10.7 | 9.4 | 0.9 | 238 | 62.4 | 462 | 122.6 |
| | 16 | 83 | 80 | 207 | 100 | 216 | 124 | 78 | 10 | 914 | 68.3 | 1.8 | 9.1 | 8.6 | 22.6 | 10.9 | 23.7 | 13.6 | 8.5 | 1.1 | 784 | 58.1 | 1698 | 126.1 |

## III. PAUSES MARKED BY COMMAS

| | ABSOLUTE FIGURES | | | | | | | | | | INTERNAL | | | | | | | | | | FINAL | | | INT. & FINAL | |
|---|---|---|---|---|---|---|---|---|---|---|---|---|---|---|---|---|---|---|---|---|---|---|---|---|---|
| | | | | | | | | | | | Per 100 Lines | PAUSES IN REL. TO EACH OTHER | | | | | | | | | | Per 100 Lines | | | Per 100 Lines |
| | 1 | 2 | 3 | 4 | 5 | 6 | 7 | 8 | 9 | Total | | 1 | 2 | 3 | 4 | 5 | 6 | 7 | 8 | 9 | All | | All | |
| Comus | 3 | 32 | 20 | 85 | 40 | 107 | 34 | 17 | 2 | 340 | 42.9 | 0.9 | 9.4 | 5.9 | 25.0 | 11.8 | 31.5 | 10.0 | 5.0 | 0.6 | 314 | 39.6 | 654 | 82.5 |
| PL I | 3 | 35 | 30 | 79 | 69 | 105 | 49 | 36 | 6 | 412 | 51.6 | 0.7 | 8.5 | 7.3 | 19.2 | 16.7 | 25.5 | 11.9 | 8.7 | 1.5 | 168 | 21.1 | 580 | 72.7 |
| II | 5 | 60 | 61 | 133 | 77 | 155 | 63 | 67 | 10 | 631 | 59.8 | 0.8 | 9.5 | 9.7 | 21.0 | 12.2 | 24.6 | 10.0 | 10.6 | 1.6 | 226 | 21.4 | 857 | 81.2 |
| III | 8 | 48 | 48 | 114 | 40 | 105 | 36 | 36 | 8 | 443 | 59.7 | 1.8 | 10.9 | 10.8 | 25.7 | 9.0 | 23.7 | 8.1 | 8.1 | 1.8 | 207 | 27.9 | 650 | 87.6 |
| IV | 7 | 62 | 62 | 145 | 69 | 164 | 57 | 48 | 6 | 620 | 61.1 | 1.1 | 10.0 | 10.0 | 23.4 | 11.1 | 26.4 | 9.2 | 7.7 | 1.0 | 245 | 24.1 | 865 | 85.2 |
| V | 11 | 59 | 64 | 139 | 57 | 168 | 63 | 63 | 9 | 633 | 70.0 | 1.7 | 9.3 | 10.1 | 22.0 | 9.0 | 26.4 | 10.0 | 10.0 | 1.4 | 201 | 22.2 | 834 | 92.2 |
| VI | 6 | 60 | 75 | 120 | 34 | 134 | 53 | 51 | 6 | 539 | 59.1 | 1.1 | 11.1 | 13.9 | 22.3 | 6.3 | 24.9 | 9.8 | 9.5 | 1.1 | 225 | 24.7 | 764 | 83.8 |
| VII | 7 | 46 | 51 | 86 | 26 | 100 | 52 | 52 | 11 | 431 | 59.1 | 1.6 | 10.7 | 11.8 | 20.0 | 6.0 | 23.2 | 12.1 | 12.1 | 2.5 | 145 | 22.7 | 576 | 90.0 |
| VIII | 9 | 37 | 55 | 103 | 27 | 105 | 63 | 53 | 4 | 456 | 70.3 | 2.0 | 8.1 | 12.1 | 22.6 | 5.9 | 23.0 | 13.8 | 11.6 | 0.9 | 175 | 27.0 | 631 | 97.3 |
| IX | 11 | 108 | 105 | 207 | 72 | 205 | 114 | 93 | 3 | 918 | 78.1 | 1.2 | 11.6 | 12.4 | 22.3 | 7.8 | 22.1 | 12.3 | 10.0 | 0.3 | 306 | 25.7 | 1224 | 102.9 |
| X | 7 | 85 | 74 | 157 | 77 | 174 | 90 | 83 | 5 | 752 | 68.1 | 0.9 | 11.3 | 9.8 | 20.9 | 10.2 | 23.1 | 12.0 | 11.0 | 0.7 | 290 | 26.3 | 1042 | 94.4 |
| XI | 7 | 75 | 60 | 137 | 50 | 130 | 73 | 51 | 6 | 589 | 65.6 | 1.2 | 12.7 | 10.2 | 23.3 | 8.5 | 22.1 | 12.4 | 8.7 | 1.0 | 218 | 24.4 | 807 | 90.0 |
| XII | 4 | 34 | 39 | 76 | 45 | 87 | 60 | 38 | 2 | 385 | 59.8 | 1.0 | 8.8 | 10.1 | 19.7 | 11.7 | 22.6 | 15.6 | 9.9 | 0.5 | 160 | 24.8 | 545 | 84.6 |
| | 85 | 709 | 734 | 1496 | 643 | 1632 | 773 | 671 | 76 | 6809 | 64.4 | 1.2 | 10.4 | 10.8 | 22.0 | 9.4 | 23.9 | 11.3 | 9.8 | 1.1 | 2566 | 24.3 | 9375 | 88.8 |
| PR I | 2 | 21 | 26 | 47 | 41 | 70 | 35 | 28 | 4 | 274 | 54.6 | 0.7 | 7.7 | 9.5 | 17.1 | 15.0 | 25.5 | 12.8 | 10.2 | 1.5 | 138 | 27.5 | 412 | 81.1 |
| II | 2 | 27 | 27 | 59 | 45 | 84 | 21 | 22 | — | 287 | 59.1 | 0.7 | 9.4 | 9.4 | 20.6 | 15.7 | 29.3 | 7.3 | 7.6 | — | 169 | 34.8 | 456 | 93.9 |
| III | 2 | 10 | 38 | 47 | 36 | 68 | 39 | 26 | — | 266 | 60.1 | 0.8 | 3.8 | 14.3 | 17.6 | 13.5 | 25.6 | 14.6 | 9.8 | — | 138 | 31.2 | 404 | 91.3 |
| IV | 4 | 28 | 38 | 84 | 48 | 103 | 46 | 33 | 6 | 390 | 61.0 | 1.0 | 7.2 | 9.7 | 21.5 | 12.3 | 26.4 | 11.8 | 8.5 | 1.5 | 232 | 36.3 | 622 | 97.3 |
| | 10 | 86 | 129 | 237 | 170 | 325 | 141 | 109 | 10 | 1217 | 58.8 | 0.8 | 7.1 | 10.6 | 19.5 | 14.0 | 26.7 | 11.6 | 9.0 | 0.8 | 677 | 32.7 | 1894 | 91.5 |
| SA (A) | 5 | 32 | 23 | 56 | 29 | 61 | 42 | 20 | 4 | 272 | 57.4 | 1.8 | 11.8 | 8.5 | 20.6 | 10.7 | 22.4 | 15.4 | 7.3 | 1.5 | 160 | 33.8 | 432 | 78.5 |
| (B) | 6 | 27 | 28 | 62 | 35 | 70 | 33 | 26 | 4 | 291 | 59.1 | 2.1 | 9.3 | 9.6 | 21.3 | 12.0 | 24.1 | 11.3 | 8.9 | 1.4 | 141 | 28.7 | 432 | 87.8 |
| (C) | 5 | 19 | 17 | 45 | 14 | 42 | 21 | 19 | 2 | 184 | 49.5 | 2.7 | 10.3 | 9.2 | 24.5 | 7.6 | 22.8 | 11.4 | 10.3 | 1.1 | 96 | 25.8 | 280 | 75.3 |
| | 16 | 78 | 68 | 163 | 78 | 173 | 96 | 65 | 10 | 747 | 55.8 | 2.1 | 10.4 | 9.1 | 21.8 | 10.4 | 23.2 | 12.9 | 8.7 | 1.4 | 397 | 29.7 | 1144 | 85.5 |

## IV. PAUSES—HEAVY PUNCTUATION MARKS

| | \| | | | | Internal | | | | | | | | | | | Final | | Final & Int. | |
|---|---|---|---|---|---|---|---|---|---|---|---|---|---|---|---|---|---|---|---|
| | 1 | 2 | 3 | 4 | 5 | 6 | 7 | 8 | 9 | Total | Per 100 Lines | 1 | 2 | 3 | 4 | 5 | 6 | 7 | 8 | 9 | All | Per 100 Lines | All | Per 100 Lines |
| Comus | — | 2 | — | 12 | 5 | 34 | 9 | 4 | 2 | 68 | 8.6 | — | 2.9 | — | 17.6 | 7.4 | 50.0 | 13.2 | 5.9 | 2.9 | 155 | 19.6 | 223 | 28.2 |
| PL I | — | 4 | 6 | 42 | 27 | 37 | 18 | 9 | — | 143 | 17.9 | — | 2.8 | 4.2 | 29.4 | 18.9 | 25.9 | 12.6 | 6.3 | — | 100 | 12.5 | 243 | 30.4 |
| II | — | 12 | 15 | 71 | 42 | 70 | 19 | 11 | — | 240 | 22.6 | — | 5.0 | 6.2 | 29.6 | 17.5 | 29.1 | 7.9 | 4.6 | — | 143 | 13.6 | 383 | 36.3 |
| III | — | 4 | 2 | 20 | 17 | 25 | 4 | 8 | — | 80 | 10.8 | — | 5.0 | 2.5 | 25.0 | 21.2 | 31.2 | 5.0 | 10.0 | — | 140 | 18.9 | 220 | 29.7 |
| IV | 1 | 8 | 12 | 61 | 22 | 55 | 7 | 9 | — | 175 | 17.2 | 0.6 | 4.6 | 6.9 | 34.9 | 12.6 | 31.4 | 4.0 | 5.1 | — | 194 | 19.1 | 369 | 36.3 |
| V | — | 3 | 10 | 42 | 23 | 52 | 11 | 15 | — | 156 | 17.3 | — | 1.9 | 6.4 | 26.9 | 14.7 | 33.3 | 7.0 | 9.7 | — | 155 | 17.1 | 311 | 34.4 |
| VI | 1 | 11 | 22 | 47 | 19 | 45 | 15 | 10 | 1 | 171 | 18.8 | 0.6 | 6.4 | 12.9 | 27.5 | 11.1 | 26.3 | 8.8 | 5.8 | 0.6 | 143 | 15.6 | 314 | 34.4 |
| VII | — | 10 | 17 | 28 | 8 | 30 | 8 | 13 | 1 | 115 | 18.0 | — | 8.7 | 14.8 | 24.3 | 6.9 | 26.1 | 6.9 | 11.3 | 0.9 | 104 | 16.2 | 219 | 34.2 |
| VIII | — | 6 | 11 | 25 | 14 | 26 | 11 | 12 | — | 105 | 16.2 | — | 5.7 | 10.5 | 23.8 | 13.3 | 24.8 | 10.5 | 11.4 | — | 138 | 21.3 | 243 | 37.5 |
| IX | 1 | 10 | 16 | 45 | 18 | 39 | 20 | 10 | — | 159 | 13.4 | 0.6 | 6.3 | 10.1 | 28.3 | 11.3 | 24.5 | 12.6 | 6.3 | — | 252 | 21.2 | 411 | 34.6 |
| X | — | 10 | 11 | 47 | 28 | 66 | 27 | 16 | — | 205 | 18.6 | — | 4.9 | 5.3 | 22.9 | 13.6 | 32.2 | 13.2 | 7.8 | — | 158 | 14.3 | 363 | 32.9 |
| XI | — | 6 | 15 | 33 | 16 | 64 | 17 | 12 | — | 163 | 18.2 | — | 3.7 | 9.2 | 20.2 | 9.8 | 39.3 | 10.4 | 7.4 | — | 174 | 19.4 | 337 | 37.6 |
| XII | — | 3 | 8 | 30 | 23 | 37 | 12 | 6 | — | 119 | 18.5 | — | 2.5 | 6.7 | 25.2 | 19.3 | 31.1 | 10.1 | 5.0 | — | 109 | 16.9 | 228 | 35.4 |
| | 3 | 87 | 145 | 491 | 257 | 546 | 169 | 131 | 2 | 1831 | 17.3 | 0.2 | 4.7 | 7.9 | 26.8 | 14.0 | 29.8 | 9.2 | 7.1 | 0.1 | 1810 | 17.2 | 3641 | 34.5 |
| PR I | — | 5 | 5 | 13 | 7 | 18 | 3 | 7 | 1 | 59 | 11.8 | — | 8.5 | 8.5 | 22.0 | 11.8 | 30.5 | 5.1 | 11.8 | 1.7 | 104 | 20.7 | 163 | 32.5 |
| II | — | 1 | 5 | 13 | 8 | 18 | 6 | 5 | 1 | 57 | 11.7 | — | 1.7 | 8.8 | 22.8 | 14.0 | 31.6 | 10.5 | 8.8 | 1.7 | 115 | 23.7 | 172 | 35.4 |
| III | — | 4 | 6 | 11 | 7 | 17 | 9 | 3 | — | 57 | 12.9 | — | 7.0 | 10.5 | 19.3 | 12.3 | 29.8 | 15.8 | 5.3 | — | 111 | 25.1 | 168 | 37.9 |
| IV | — | 3 | 8 | 23 | 13 | 20 | 6 | 2 | — | 75 | 11.7 | — | 4.0 | 10.7 | 30.7 | 17.3 | 26.7 | 8.0 | 2.7 | — | 137 | 21.4 | 212 | 33.2 |
| | — | 13 | 24 | 60 | 35 | 73 | 24 | 17 | 2 | 248 | 12.0 | — | 5.2 | 9.7 | 24.2 | 14.1 | 29.4 | 9.7 | 6.8 | 0.8 | 467 | 22.6 | 715 | 34.5 |
| SA (A) | — | 1 | 6 | 19 | 10 | 22 | 15 | 9 | — | 82 | 17.3 | — | 1.2 | 7.3 | 23.2 | 12.2 | 26.8 | 18.3 | 11.0 | — | 108 | 22.8 | 190 | 40.1 |
| (B) | — | — | 2 | 15 | 6 | 10 | 10 | 2 | — | 45 | 9.1 | — | — | 4.4 | 33.3 | 13.3 | 22.2 | 22.2 | 4.4 | — | 137 | 27.8 | 182 | 36.9 |
| (C) | — | 4 | 4 | 10 | 6 | 11 | 3 | 2 | — | 40 | 10.8 | — | 10.0 | 10.0 | 25.0 | 15.0 | 27.5 | 7.5 | 5.0 | — | 136 | 36.5 | 176 | 36.5 |
| | — | 5 | 12 | 44 | 22 | 43 | 28 | 13 | — | 167 | 12.5 | — | 3.0 | 7.2 | 26.3 | 13.2 | 25.7 | 16.8 | 7.8 | — | 381 | 28.5 | 548 | 41.0 |

## V. PAUSES

| | a : m : b | | | $e^1 : \mu : e^2$ | | |
|---|---|---|---|---|---|---|
| | All punct. marks | Commas | Heavy punct. marks | All punct. marks | Commas | Heavy punct. marks |
| Comus | 37.7 : 11.0 : 51.2 | 41.2 : 11.8 : 47.0 | 20.6 : 7.4 : 72.0 | 14.0 : 69.4 : 16.6 | 16.2 : 68.2 : 15.6 | 2.9 : 75.0 : 22.1 |
| PL I | 35.9 : 17.3 : 46.8 | 35.7 : 16.7 : 47.6 | 36.4 : 18.9 : 44.7 | 14.0 : 64.7 : 21.2 | 16.5 : 61.4 : 22.1 | 7.0 : 74.1 : 18.9 |
| II | 41.0 : 13.7 : 45.3 | 41.0 : 12.2 : 46.8 | 40.8 : 17.5 : 41.6 | 17.6 : 62.9 : 19.5 | 20.0 : 57.8 : 22.2 | 11.25 : 76.25 : 12.5 |
| III | 46.7 : 10.9 : 42.4 | 49.2 : 9.0 : 41.8 | 32.5 : 21.2 : 46.2 | 21.0 : 61.4 : 17.6 | 23.5 : 58.5 : 18.0 | 7.5 : 77.5 : 15.0 |
| IV | 45.0 : 11.5 : 43.5 | 44.5 : 11.1 : 44.4 | 46.9 : 12.6 : 40.5 | 19.1 : 64.9 : 16.0 | 21.1 : 61.0 : 17.9 | 12.0 : 78.9 : 9.1 |
| V | 41.6 : 10.1 : 48.3 | 43.1 : 9.0 : 47.9 | 35.2 : 14.7 : 50.0 | 18.6 : 61.0 : 20.4 | 21.2 : 57.5 : 21.3 | 8.3 : 75.0 : 16.7 |
| VI | 48.2 : 7.4 : 44.4 | 48.4 : 6.3 : 45.3 | 47.4 : 11.1 : 41.5 | 24.6 : 56.2 : 19.1 | 26.2 : 53.4 : 20.4 | 19.9 : 64.9 : 15.2 |
| VII | 44.9 : 6.2 : 48.9 | 44.1 : 6.0 : 49.9 | 47.8 : 6.9 : 45.2 | 24.0 : 50.9 : 25.1 | 24.1 : 49.2 : 26.7 | 23.5 : 57.4 : 19.0 |
| VIII | 43.9 : 7.3 : 48.8 | 44.8 : 5.9 : 49.3 | 40.0 : 13.3 : 46.7 | 21.0 : 53.5 : 25.5 | 22.2 : 51.5 : 26.3 | 16.2 : 61.9 : 21.9 |
| IX | 46.7 : 8.4 : 44.9 | 47.5 : 7.7 : 44.7 | 45.3 : 11.3 : 43.4 | 23.3 : 54.4 : 22.3 | 25.2 : 52.2 : 22.6 | 17.0 : 64.1 : 18.9 |
| X | 40.9 : 11.0 : 48.1 | 43.0 : 10.2 : 46.8 | 33.1 : 13.6 : 53.2 | 19.5 : 57.4 : 23.1 | 22.1 : 54.2 : 23.7 | 10.2 : 68.8 : 21.0 |
| XI | 44.3 : 8.8 : 46.9 | 47.5 : 8.5 : 44.0 | 33.1 : 9.8 : 57.1 | 21.7 : 57.2 : 21.1 | 24.1 : 53.9 : 22.0 | 12.9 : 69.3 : 17.8 |
| XII | 38.5 : 13.5 : 48.0 | 39.7 : 11.7 : 48.6 | 34.4 : 19.3 : 46.2 | 17.5 : 59.1 : 23.4 | 20.0 : 54.0 : 26.0 | 9.3 : 75.6 : 15.1 |
| | 43.3 : 10.4 : 46.3 | 44.3 : 9.4 : 46.2 | 39.6 : 14.0 : 46.3 | 20.3 : 58.6 : 21.1 | 22.5 : 55.2 : 22.3 | 12.8 : 70.7 : 16.5 |
| PR I | 35.7 : 14.4 : 49.9 | 35.0 : 15.0 : 50.0 | 39.0 : 11.8 : 49.1 | 17.7 : 58.9 : 23.4 | 17.9 : 57.7 : 24.4 | 17.0 : 64.4 : 18.6 |
| II | 38.9 : 15.4 : 45.6 | 40.1 : 15.7 : 44.2 | 33.3 : 14.0 : 52.6 | 18.0 : 66.0 : 16.0 | 19.5 : 65.5 : 15.0 | 10.5 : 68.4 : 21.1 |
| III | 36.5 : 13.3 : 50.2 | 36.5 : 13.5 : 50.0 | 36.8 : 12.3 : 50.9 | 18.6 : 57.6 : 23.8 | 18.8 : 56.8 : 24.4 | 17.5 : 61.4 : 21.1 |
| IV | 40.4 : 13.1 : 46.5 | 39.5 : 12.3 : 48.2 | 45.3 : 17.3 : 37.3 | 17.4 : 62.6 : 20.0 | 18.0 : 60.2 : 21.8 | 14.7 : 74.7 : 10.7 |
| | 38.2 : 14.0 : 47.8 | 38.0 : 14.0 : 48.0 | 39.1 : 14.1 : 46.8 | 17.9 : 61.4 : 20.7 | 18.5 : 60.1 : 21.4 | 14.9 : 67.8 : 17.3 |
| SA (A) | 40.1 : 11.0 : 48.9 | 42.6 : 10.7 : 46.7 | 31.8 : 12.2 : 56.0 | 18.9 : 55.6 : 25.4 | 22.1 : 53.7 : 24.2 | 8.5 : 62.2 : 29.3 |
| (B) | 41.6 : 12.2 : 46.1 | 42.3 : 12.0 : 45.7 | 37.8 : 13.3 : 48.9 | 18.8 : 58.9 : 22.3 | 21.0 : 57.4 : 21.6 | 4.4 : 68.9 : 26.7 |
| (C) | 46.4 : 8.9 : 44.6 | 46.7 : 7.6 : 45.7 | 45.0 : 15.0 : 40.0 | 21.9 : 57.1 : 21.0 | 22.3 : 54.9 : 22.8 | 20.0 : 67.5 : 12.5 |
| | 42.2 : 10.9 : 46.8 | 43.5 : 10.4 : 46.1 | 36.5 : 13.2 : 50.3 | 19.6 : 57.2 : 23.2 | 21.7 : 55.4 : 22.9 | 10.2 : 65.3 : 24.6 |

## VI. PAUSES
### ALL PUNCTUATION MARKS (according to position within line)

| | 1 | 2 | 3 | 4 | 5 | 6 | 7 | 8 | 9 | Total |
|---|---|---|---|---|---|---|---|---|---|---|
| | \multicolumn{10}{c}{Absolute Figures} | | | | | | | | | |
| PL I-II | 8 | 111 | 112 | 325 | 215 | 367 | 149 | 123 | 16 | 1426 |
| III-IV | 16 | 122 | 124 | 340 | 148 | 349 | 104 | 101 | 14 | 1318 |
| V-VI | 18 | 133 | 171 | 348 | 133 | 399 | 142 | 139 | 16 | 1499 |
| VII-VIII | 16 | 99 | 134 | 242 | 75 | 261 | 134 | 130 | 16 | 1107 |
| IX-X | 19 | 213 | 206 | 456 | 195 | 484 | 251 | 202 | 8 | 2034 |
| XI-XII | 11 | 118 | 122 | 276 | 134 | 318 | 162 | 107 | 8 | 1256 |
| | \multicolumn{10}{c}{Positions in rel. to each other} | | | | | | | | | |
| PL I-II | 0.6 | 7.8 | 7.8 | 22.8 | 15.1 | 25.7 | 10.5 | 8.6 | 1.1 | |
| III-IV | 1.2 | 9.3 | 9.4 | 25.8 | 11.2 | 26.5 | 7.9 | 7.6 | 1.1 | |
| V-VI | 1.2 | 8.9 | 11.4 | 23.2 | 8.9 | 26.6 | 9.5 | 9.3 | 1.1 | |
| VII-VIII | 1.5 | 8.9 | 12.1 | 21.9 | 6.8 | 23.6 | 12.1 | 11.7 | 1.4 | |
| IX-X | 0.9 | 10.5 | 10.1 | 22.5 | 9.6 | 23.8 | 12.3 | 9.9 | 0.4 | |
| XI-XII | 0.8 | 9.4 | 9.7 | 22.0 | 10.7 | 25.3 | 12.9 | 8.5 | 0.6 | |

# VII. PAUSES
## *Paradise Lost* (Gilbert's rearrangement)
### ALL PUNCTUATION MARKS

|  |  | \multicolumn{9}{c}{Internal} |  |  |  | Final |  | Final & Int. |  |
|---|---|---|---|---|---|---|---|---|---|---|---|---|---|---|---|---|---|
|  |  | \multicolumn{9}{c}{Absolute Figures} | Total | Per 100 Lines | \multicolumn{8}{c}{Positions in rel. to each other} | Total | Per 100 Lines | Total | Per 100 Lines |
|  | 1 | 2 | 3 | 4 | 5 | 6 | 7 | 8 | 9 | | | 1 | 2 | 3 | 4 | 5 | 6 | 7 | 8 | 9 | | | | |

| | 1 | 2 | 3 | 4 | 5 | 6 | 7 | 8 | 9 | Total | Per 100 Lines | 1 | 2 | 3 | 4 | 5 | 6 | 7 | 8 | 9 | Total | Per 100 Lines | Total | Per 100 Lines |
|---|---|---|---|---|---|---|---|---|---|---|---|---|---|---|---|---|---|---|---|---|---|---|---|---|
| Group I 13 | 130 | 111 | 308 | 147 | 335 | 157 | 110 | 7 | 1318 | 85.1 | 1.0 | 9.9 | 8.4 | 23.4 | 11.2 | 25.4 | 11.9 | 8.4 | 0.5 | 696 | 44.9 | 2014 | 130.0 |
| II 3 | 34 | 41 | 98 | 42 | 111 | 45 | 28 | 2 | 404 | 82.3 | 0.7 | 8.4 | 10.1 | 24.3 | 10.4 | 27.5 | 11.1 | 6.9 | 0.5 | 228 | 46.4 | 632 | 128.7 |
| III 10 | 56 | 57 | 174 | 73 | 169 | 66 | 64 | 5 | 674 | 82.5 | 1.5 | 8.3 | 8.5 | 25.9 | 10.9 | 25.1 | 9.8 | 9.5 | 0.7 | 336 | 41.1 | 1010 | 123.6 |
| IV 21 | 223 | 262 | 489 | 150 | 500 | 260 | 216 | 20 | 2141 | 87.7 | 1.0 | 10.4 | 12.2 | 22.8 | 7.0 | 23.4 | 12.1 | 10.1 | 0.9 | 1082 | 44.4 | 3223 | 132.0 |
| V 17 | 156 | 176 | 421 | 221 | 524 | 197 | 179 | 18 | 1909 | 76.4 | 0.9 | 8.2 | 9.2 | 22.1 | 11.6 | 27.4 | 10.3 | 9.4 | 0.9 | 956 | 38.2 | 2865 | 114.6 |
| VI 24 | 197 | 222 | 497 | 267 | 539 | 217 | 205 | 26 | 2194 | 79.2 | 1.1 | 9.0 | 10.1 | 22.6 | 12.2 | 24.6 | 9.9 | 9.3 | 1.2 | 1078 | 38.9 | 3272 | 118.2 |
| 88 | 796 | 869 | 1987 | 900 | 2178 | 942 | 802 | 78 | 8640 | 81.8 | 1.0 | 9.2 | 10.1 | 23.0 | 10.4 | 25.2 | 10.9 | 9.3 | 0.9 | 4376 | 41.5 | 13016 | 123.4 |

### Commas

| | 1 | 2 | 3 | 4 | 5 | 6 | 7 | 8 | 9 | Total | Per 100 Lines | 1 | 2 | 3 | 4 | 5 | 6 | 7 | 8 | 9 | Total | Per 100 Lines | Total | Per 100 Lines |
|---|---|---|---|---|---|---|---|---|---|---|---|---|---|---|---|---|---|---|---|---|---|---|---|---|
| Group I 12 | 114 | 93 | 228 | 106 | 226 | 121 | 91 | 7 | 998 | 64.4 | 1.2 | 11.4 | 9.3 | 22.8 | 10.6 | 22.6 | 12.1 | 9.1 | 0.7 | 416 | 26.9 | 1414 | 91.3 |
| II 3 | 33 | 28 | 78 | 28 | 73 | 34 | 25 | 2 | 304 | 61.9 | 1.0 | 10.9 | 9.2 | 25.7 | 9.2 | 24.0 | 11.2 | 8.2 | 0.7 | 137 | 27.9 | 441 | 89.8 |
| III 10 | 54 | 51 | 137 | 28 | 139 | 59 | 52 | 5 | 564 | 69.0 | 1.8 | 9.6 | 9.0 | 24.3 | 10.1 | 24.6 | 10.5 | 9.2 | 0.9 | 211 | 25.8 | 775 | 94.8 |
| IV 20 | 196 | 225 | 377 | 105 | 389 | 217 | 182 | 18 | 1729 | 70.5 | 1.2 | 11.3 | 13.0 | 21.8 | 6.1 | 22.5 | 12.6 | 10.5 | 1.0 | 604 | 24.8 | 2323 | 95.2 |
| V 17 | 136 | 156 | 310 | 159 | 412 | 162 | 147 | 18 | 1517 | 60.7 | 1.1 | 9.0 | 10.3 | 20.4 | 10.5 | 27.2 | 10.7 | 9.7 | 1.2 | 551 | 22.0 | 2068 | 82.7 |
| VI 23 | 176 | 181 | 366 | 188 | 393 | 180 | 174 | 26 | 1707 | 61.6 | 1.3 | 10.3 | 10.6 | 21.5 | 11.0 | 23.0 | 10.6 | 10.2 | 1.5 | 647 | 23.4 | 2354 | 85.0 |
| 85 | 709 | 734 | 1496 | 643 | 1632 | 773 | 671 | 76 | 6809 | 64.4 | 1.2 | 10.4 | 10.8 | 22.0 | 9.4 | 23.9 | 11.3 | 9.8 | 1.1 | 2566 | 24.3 | 9375 | 88.8 |

### Heavy Punctuation Marks

| | 1 | 2 | 3 | 4 | 5 | 6 | 7 | 8 | 9 | Total | Per 100 Lines | 1 | 2 | 3 | 4 | 5 | 6 | 7 | 8 | 9 | Total | Per 100 Lines | Total | Per 100 Lines |
|---|---|---|---|---|---|---|---|---|---|---|---|---|---|---|---|---|---|---|---|---|---|---|---|---|
| Group I 1 | 16 | 18 | 80 | 41 | 109 | 36 | 19 | — | 320 | 20.6 | 0.3 | 5.0 | 5.6 | 25.0 | 12.8 | 34.1 | 11.3 | 5.9 | — | 280 | 18.1 | 600 | 38.7 |
| II — | 1 | 13 | 20 | 14 | 38 | 11 | 3 | — | 100 | 20.4 | — | 1.0 | 13.0 | 20.0 | 14.0 | 38.0 | 11.0 | 3.0 | — | 91 | 18.5 | 191 | 38.9 |
| III — | 2 | 6 | 37 | 16 | 30 | 7 | 12 | — | 110 | 13.5 | — | 1.8 | 5.5 | 33.6 | 14.5 | 27.3 | 6.4 | 10.9 | — | 125 | 15.3 | 235 | 28.8 |
| IV 1 | 27 | 47 | 112 | 45 | 111 | 43 | 34 | 2 | 422 | 17.3 | 0.2 | 6.4 | 11.1 | 26.5 | 10.7 | 26.3 | 10.2 | 8.1 | 0.5 | 478 | 19.6 | 900 | 36.9 |
| V — | 20 | 20 | 111 | 62 | 112 | 35 | 32 | — | 392 | 15.7 | — | 5.1 | 5.1 | 28.3 | 15.8 | 28.6 | 8.9 | 8.2 | — | 405 | 16.2 | 797 | 31.9 |
| VI 1 | 21 | 41 | 131 | 79 | 146 | 37 | 31 | — | 487 | 17.6 | 0.2 | 4.3 | 8.5 | 26.9 | 16.2 | 30.0 | 7.6 | 6.3 | — | 431 | 15.6 | 918 | 33.2 |
| 3 | 87 | 145 | 491 | 257 | 546 | 169 | 131 | 2 | 1831 | 17.3 | 0.2 | 4.7 | 7.9 | 26.8 | 14.0 | 29.8 | 9.2 | 7.1 | 0.1 | 1810 | 17.2 | 3641 | 34.5 |

## VIII. PAUSES
### Per 100 Lines

| | All punct. marks | Total | a + m + b Commas | Total | Heavy punct. marks | Total | All punct. marks | Commas | $e^1 + \mu + e^2$ Heavy punct. marks |
|---|---|---|---|---|---|---|---|---|---|
| *Comus* | 19.4 + 5.7 + 26.4 | 51.5 | 17.6 + 5.1 + 20.2 | 42.9 | 1.8 + 0.6 + 6.2 | 8.6 | 7.2 + 35.7 + 8.6 | 6.9 + 29.3 + 6.7 | 0.3 + 6.4 + 1.9 |
| *PL* I | 24.9 + 12.0 + 32.6 | 69.5 | 18.4 + 8.6 + 24.5 | 51.6 | 6.5 + 3.4 + 8.0 | 17.9 | 9.7 + 45.0 + 14.8 | 8.5 + 31.7 + 11.4 | 1.2 + 13.3 + 3.4 |
| II | 33.9 + 11.3 + 37.4 | 82.6 | 24.5 + 7.3 + 28.0 | 59.8 | 9.3 + 4.0 + 9.5 | 22.8 | 14.5 + 52.0 + 16.1 | 11.9 + 34.6 + 13.3 | 2.6 + 17.4 + 2.8 |
| III | 32.9 + 7.7 + 29.9 | 70.5 | 29.5 + 5.4 + 24.9 | 59.7 | 3.5 + 2.3 + 5.0 | 10.8 | 14.8 + 43.3 + 12.4 | 14.0 + 34.9 + 10.8 | 0.8 + 8.4 + 1.6 |
| IV | 35.3 + 9.0 + 34.1 | 78.4 | 27.2 + 6.8 + 27.1 | 61.1 | 8.1 + 2.2 + 7.0 | 17.3 | 15.0 + 50.8 + 12.5 | 12.9 + 37.2 + 11.0 | 2.1 + 13.6 + 1.6 |
| V | 36.3 + 8.9 + 42.1 | 87.3 | 30.2 + 6.3 + 33.5 | 70.0 | 6.1 + 2.6 + 8.6 | 17.3 | 16.2 + 53.3 + 17.8 | 14.8 + 40.3 + 14.9 | 1.5 + 12.9 + 2.9 |
| VI | 37.5 + 5.8 + 34.5 | 77.8 | 28.6 + 3.7 + 26.8 | 59.1 | 8.9 + 2.1 + 7.7 | 18.7 | 19.2 + 43.7 + 14.9 | 15.4 + 31.6 + 12.1 | 3.7 + 12.2 + 2.9 |
| VII | 38.3 + 5.3 + 41.7 | 85.3 | 29.6 + 4.1 + 33.6 | 67.3 | 8.6 + 1.3 + 8.1 | 18.0 | 20.5 + 43.4 + 21.4 | 16.2 + 33.1 + 18.0 | 4.2 + 10.3 + 3.5 |
| VIII | 37.9 + 6.3 + 42.2 | 86.4 | 31.4 + 4.2 + 34.7 | 70.3 | 6.5 + 2.1 + 7.5 | 16.1 | 18.2 + 46.2 + 22.0 | 15.6 + 36.2 + 18.5 | 2.6 + 10.0 + 3.5 |
| IX | 42.3 + 7.6 + 40.7 | 90.6 | 36.2 + 6.1 + 34.9 | 77.2 | 6.1 + 1.5 + 5.8 | 13.4 | 21.1 + 49.3 + 20.2 | 18.8 + 40.7 + 17.7 | 2.3 + 8.6 + 2.5 |
| X | 35.4 + 9.5 + 41.8 | 86.7 | 29.1 + 7.0 + 31.9 | 68.0 | 6.2 + 2.6 + 9.9 | 18.7 | 17.0 + 49.7 + 20.0 | 15.0 + 37.0 + 16.1 | 1.9 + 12.8 + 3.9 |
| XI | 37.1 + 7.4 + 39.4 | 83.9 | 31.1 + 5.6 + 28.9 | 65.6 | 6.0 + 1.8 + 10.4 | 18.3 | 18.2 + 47.9 + 17.7 | 15.8 + 35.4 + 14.4 | 2.4 + 12.6 + 3.2 |
| XII | 30.1 + 10.6 + 37.6 | 78.3 | 23.8 + 7.0 + 29.0 | 59.8 | 6.4 + 3.6 + 8.5 | 18.5 | 13.7 + 46.3 + 18.3 | 12.0 + 32.3 + 15.5 | 1.7 + 14.0 + 2.8 |
| | 35.5 + 8.5 + 37.9 | 81.9 | 28.5 + 6.1 + 29.8 | 64.4 | 6.9 + 2.4 + 8.1 | 17.4 | 16.6 + 48.0 + 17.3 | 14.4 + 35.7 + 14.4 | 2.2 + 12.2 + 3.0 |
| *PR* I | 23.7 + 9.6 + 33.0 | 66.3 | 19.1 + 8.2 + 27.3 | 54.6 | 4.6 + 1.4 + 5.7 | 11.7 | 11.8 + 39.0 + 15.5 | 9.8 + 31.5 + 13.3 | 2.0 + 7.6 + 2.2 |
| II | 27.6 + 10.9 + 32.3 | 70.8 | 23.7 + 9.3 + 26.0 | 59.0 | 3.9 + 1.7 + 6.2 | 11.8 | 12.8 + 46.7 + 11.3 | 11.5 + 38.7 + 8.8 | 1.2 + 8.0 + 2.5 |
| III | 26.6 + 9.7 + 36.6 | 72.9 | 21.9 + 8.1 + 30.0 | 60.0 | 4.7 + 1.6 + 6.6 | 12.9 | 13.5 + 42.0 + 17.4 | 11.3 + 34.1 + 14.6 | 2.3 + 7.9 + 2.7 |
| IV | 29.4 + 9.5 + 33.8 | 72.7 | 24.1 + 7.5 + 29.4 | 61.0 | 5.3 + 2.0 + 4.4 | 11.7 | 12.7 + 45.5 + 14.6 | 10.9 + 36.8 + 13.3 | 1.7 + 8.8 + 1.2 |
| | 27.0 + 9.9 + 33.9 | 70.8 | 22.3 + 8.2 + 28.3 | 58.8 | 4.7 + 1.7 + 5.6 | 12.0 | 12.7 + 43.5 + 14.6 | 10.9 + 35.4 + 12.5 | 1.8 + 8.1 + 2.1 |
| *SA* (A) | 30.0 + 8.2 + 36.5 | 74.7 | 24.5 + 6.1 + 26.8 | 57.4 | 5.5 + 2.1 + 9.7 | 17.3 | 14.1 + 41.6 + 19.0 | 12.7 + 30.8 + 13.9 | 1.5 + 10.8 + 5.0 |
| (B) | 28.5 + 8.3 + 31.5 | 68.3 | 25.0 + 7.1 + 27.0 | 59.1 | 3.5 + 1.2 + 4.5 | 9.1 | 12.8 + 40.2 + 15.4 | 12.4 + 33.9 + 12.8 | 0.4 + 6.3 + 2.4 |
| (C) | 27.9 + 5.4 + 26.9 | 60.2 | 23.1 + 3.8 + 22.6 | 49.5 | 4.8 + 1.6 + 4.3 | 10.7 | 13.2 + 34.4 + 12.6 | 11.0 + 27.1 + 11.3 | 2.2 + 7.2 + 1.3 |
| | 28.8 + 7.5 + 32.0 | 68.3 | 24.3 + 5.8 + 25.7 | 55.8 | 4.6 + 1.6 + 6.3 | 12.5 | 13.4 + 39.1 + 15.8 | 12.1 + 30.9 + 12.8 | 1.3 + 8.2 + 3.1 |

## IX. PAUSES
### Per 100 Lines

|  | All punct. marks | | | Total | Commas | | | Total | Heavy punct. marks | | | Total |
|---|---|---|---|---|---|---|---|---|---|---|---|---|
|  | \multicolumn{4}{c}{} | \multicolumn{4}{c}{a + m + b} | | | | | |

| | All punct. marks | | | Total | Commas | | | Total | Heavy punct. marks | | | Total |
|---|---|---|---|---|---|---|---|---|---|---|---|---|
| *PL* I-II   | 30.0 + | 11.6 + | 35.3 | 77.0 | 21.9 + | 7.9 + | 26.5 | 56.3 | 8.1 + | 3.7 + | 8.9  | 20.7 |
| III-IV      | 34.1 + | 8.4 +  | 32.1 | 74.6 | 28.0 + | 6.2 + | 26.0 | 60.2 | 6.1 + | 2.2 + | 6.1  | 14.4 |
| V-VI        | 36.8 + | 7.3 +  | 38.3 | 82.5 | 29.4 + | 5.0 + | 30.1 | 64.5 | 7.5 + | 2.3 + | 8.2  | 18.0 |
| VII-VIII    | 38.1 + | 5.8 +  | 42.0 | 85.9 | 30.6 + | 4.1 + | 34.1 | 68.8 | 7.5 + | 1.7 + | 7.9  | 17.1 |
| IX-X        | 39.0 + | 8.5 +  | 41.2 | 88.7 | 32.9 + | 6.6 + | 33.4 | 72.8 | 6.1 + | 2.0 + | 7.8  | 15.9 |
| XI-XII      | 34.2 + | 8.7 +  | 38.6 | 81.5 | 28.0 + | 6.2 + | 28.9 | 63.1 | 6.3 + | 2.5 + | 9.6  | 18.4 |

$e^1 + \mu + e^2$

| | | | | | | | | | | | | |
|---|---|---|---|---|---|---|---|---|---|---|---|---|
| *PL* I-II   | 12.6 + | 48.9 + | 15.5 | 77.0 | 10.5 + | 33.4 + | 12.4 | 56.3 | 2.0 + | 15.6 + | 3.1  | 20.7 |
| III-IV      | 14.8 + | 47.4 + | 12.4 | 74.6 | 13.3 + | 36.1 + | 10.8 | 60.2 | 1.5 + | 11.3 + | 1.6  | 14.4 |
| V-VI        | 17.6 + | 48.5 + | 16.4 | 82.5 | 15.1 + | 35.9 + | 13.5 | 64.5 | 2.6 + | 12.5 + | 2.9  | 18.0 |
| VII-VIII    | 19.3 + | 44.9 + | 21.7 | 85.9 | 15.9 + | 34.7 + | 18.2 | 68.8 | 3.4 + | 10.2 + | 3.5  | 17.1 |
| IX-X        | 19.1 + | 49.5 + | 20.1 | 88.7 | 17.0 + | 38.9 + | 16.9 | 72.8 | 2.1 + | 10.6 + | 3.2  | 15.9 |
| XI-XII      | 16.3 + | 47.2 + | 18.0 | 81.5 | 14.2 + | 34.2 + | 14.8 | 63.2 | 2.1 + | 13.2 + | 3.0  | 18.3 |

*PL* (Gilbert's Rearrangement)

a + m + b

| | | | | | | | | | | | | |
|---|---|---|---|---|---|---|---|---|---|---|---|---|
| Group I   | 36.3 + | 9.5 + | 39.3 | 85.1 | 28.9 + | 6.8 + | 28.7 | 64.4 | 7.4 + | 2.6 + | 10.6 | 20.6 |
| II        | 35.8 + | 8.6 + | 37.9 | 82.3 | 28.9 + | 5.7 + | 27.3 | 61.9 | 6.9 + | 2.9 + | 10.6 | 20.4 |
| III       | 36.4 + | 8.9 + | 37.2 | 82.5 | 30.8 + | 7.0 + | 31.2 | 69.0 | 5.5 + | 1.8 + | 6.0  | 13.5 |
| IV        | 40.8 + | 6.1 + | 40.8 | 87.8 | 33.1 + | 4.4 + | 33.0 | 70.5 | 7.7 + | 1.8 + | 7.8  | 17.3 |
| V         | 30.8 + | 8.9 + | 36.7 | 76.4 | 24.8 + | 6.3 + | 29.6 | 60.7 | 6.0 + | 2.5 + | 7.2  | 15.7 |
| VI        | 34.0 + | 9.6 + | 35.6 | 79.4 | 26.9 + | 6.7 + | 28.0 | 61.6 | 7.0 + | 2.9 + | 7.7  | 17.6 |

$e^1 + \mu + e^2$

| | | | | | | | | | | | | |
|---|---|---|---|---|---|---|---|---|---|---|---|---|
| Group I   | 16.4 + | 51.0 + | 17.7 | 85.1 | 14.1 + | 36.1 + | 14.1 | 64.4 | 2.3 + | 14.8 + | 3.5 | 20.6 |
| II        | 15.9 + | 51.1 + | 15.3 | 82.3 | 13.0 + | 36.5 + | 12.4 | 61.9 | 2.9 + | 14.6 + | 2.9 | 20.4 |
| III       | 15.1 + | 50.9 + | 16.5 | 82.5 | 14.1 + | 40.7 + | 14.2 | 69.0 | 1.0 + | 10.2 + | 2.3 | 13.5 |
| IV        | 20.8 + | 46.7 + | 20.3 | 87.8 | 17.7 + | 35.7 + | 17.1 | 70.5 | 3.1 + | 11.0 + | 3.2 | 17.3 |
| V         | 14.0 + | 46.6 + | 15.8 | 76.4 | 12.4 + | 35.2 + | 13.1 | 60.7 | 1.6 + | 11.4 + | 2.7 | 15.7 |
| VI        | 16.0 + | 47.0 + | 16.2 | 79.2 | 13.7 + | 34.2 + | 13.7 | 61.6 | 2.2 + | 12.9 + | 2.5 | 17.6 |

## X. PAUSES

|  | All punct. marks | a : m : b<br>Commas | Heavy punct. marks |
|---|---|---|---|
| PL I-II | 39.0 : 15.1 : 45.9 | 38.9 : 14.0 : 47.1 | 39.2 : 18.0 : 42.7 |
| III-IV | 45.7 : 11.2 : 43.1 | 46.5 : 10.3 : 43.2 | 42.3 : 15.3 : 42.3 |
| V-VI | 44.7 : 8.9 : 46.4 | 45.5 : 7.8 : 46.7 | 41.6 : 12.8 : 45.6 |
| VII-VIII | 44.4 : 6.8 : 48.8 | 44.4 : 6.0 : 49.6 | 44.1 : 10.0 : 41.9 |
| IX-X | 43.9 : 9.6 : 46.5 | 45.2 : 8.9 : 45.9 | 38.5 : 12.6 : 48.9 |
| XI-XII | 41.9 : 10.7 : 47.4 | 44.4 : 9.8 : 45.8 | 33.7 : 13.8 : 52.5 |

|  |  | $e^1 : \mu : e^2$ |  |
|---|---|---|---|
| PL I-II | 16.2 : 63.6 : 20.2 | 18.6 : 59.3 : 22.1 | 9.7 : 75.5 : 14.8 |
| III-IV | 19.9 : 63.5 : 16.6 | 22.1 : 59.9 : 18.0 | 10.6 : 78.4 : 11.0 |
| V-VI | 21.5 : 58.7 : 19.8 | 23.4 : 55.7 : 20.9 | 14.4 : 69.7 : 15.9 |
| VII-VIII | 22.5 : 52.2 : 25.3 | 23.1 : 50.4 : 26.5 | 20.0 : 59.5 : 20.5 |
| IX-X | 21.5 : 55.8 : 22.7 | 23.4 : 53.4 : 23.2 | 13.2 : 66.7 : 20.1 |
| XI-XII | 20.0 : 57.9 : 22.1 | 22.5 : 53.9 : 23.5 | 11.3 : 72.0 : 16.7 |

|  |  | PL (Gilbert's Rearrangement)<br>a : m : b |  |
|---|---|---|---|
| Group I | 42.6 : 11.2 : 46.2 | 44.7 : 10.6 : 44.6 | 35.9 : 12.8 : 51.3 |
| II | 43.6 : 10.4 : 46.0 | 46.7 : 9.2 : 44.1 | 34.0 : 14.0 : 52.0 |
| III | 44.1 : 10.9 : 45.0 | 44.7 : 10.1 : 45.2 | 40.9 : 14.5 : 44.6 |
| IV | 46.5 : 7 0 : 46.5 | 47.0 : 6.1 : 46.9 | 44.3 : 10.7 : 45.0 |
| V | 40.3 : 11.6 : 48.1 | 40.8 : 10.5 : 48.7 | 38.5 : 15.8 : 45.7 |
| VI | 42.8 : 12.2 : 45.0 | 43.7 : 11.0 : 45.3 | 39.8 : 16.2 : 44.0 |

|  |  | $e^1 : \mu : e^2$ |  |
|---|---|---|---|
| Group I | 19.3 : 59.9 : 20.8 | 21.9 : 56.1 : 21.9 | 10.9 : 71.9 : 17.2 |
| II | 19.3 : 62.1 : 18.6 | 21.0 : 58.9 : 20.1 | 14.0 : 72.0 : 14.0 |
| III | 18.3 : 61.8 : 19.9 | 20.4 : 59.0 : 20.6 | 7.3 : 75.4 : 17.3 |
| IV | 23.6 : 53.2 : 23.2 | 25.1 : 50.7 : 24.2 | 17.8 : 63.5 : 18.7 |
| V | 18.3 : 61.1 : 20.6 | 20.3 : 58.1 : 21.6 | 10.2 : 72.7 : 17.1 |
| VI | 20.2 : 59.4 : 20.4 | 22.3 : 55.4 : 22.3 | 12.9 : 73.1 : 14.0 |

## XI. PAUSES

| | Final : internal | | | a : b | | | $e^1 : e^2$ | | | % of odd positions | | |
|---|---|---|---|---|---|---|---|---|---|---|---|---|
| | All punct. marks | Commas | Heavy punct. marks | All punct. marks | Commas | Heavy punct. marks | All punct. marks | Commas | Heavy punct. marks | All punct. marks | Commas | Heavy punct. marks |
| *Comus* | 53.5 : 46.5 | 48.0 : 52.0 | 69.5 : 30.5 | 42.4 : 57.6 | 46.7 : 53.3 | 22.2 : 77.8 | 45.6 : 54.4 | 50.9 : 49.1 | 11.8 : 88.2 | 28.6 | 29.1 | 23.5 |
| *PL* I | 32.6 : 67.4 | 29.0 : 71.0 | 41.2 : 58.8 | 43.4 : 56.6 | 42.6 : 57.4 | 44.8 : 55.2 | 39.8 : 60.2 | 42.8 : 57.2 | 27.0 : 73.0 | 37.3 | 35.2 | 35.7 |
| II | 30.0 : 70.0 | 26.4 : 73.6 | 37.3 : 62.7 | 47.5 : 52.5 | 46.8 : 53.2 | 49.4 : 50.6 | 47.4 : 52.6 | 47.6 : 52.4 | 47.4 : 52.6 | 33.5 | 34.2 | 31.7 |
| III | 40.2 : 59.8 | 31.8 : 68.2 | 63.6 : 36.4 | 52.4 : 47.6 | 54.1 : 45.9 | 41.3 : 58.7 | 54.5 : 45.5 | 56.5 : 43.5 | 33.3 : 66.7 | 31.2 | 31.6 | 27.5 |
| IV | 32.9 : 67.1 | 28.3 : 71.7 | 52.6 : 47.4 | 50.9 : 49.1 | 50.1 : 49.9 | 53.6 : 46.3 | 54.5 : 45.5 | 50.4 : 49.6 | 56.8 : 43.2 | 30.6 | 32.4 | 24.0 |
| V | 31.1 : 68.9 | 24.1 : 75.9 | 49.8 : 50.2 | 46.3 : 53.7 | 47.4 : 52.6 | 41.4 : 58.6 | 47.7 : 52.3 | 49.8 : 50.2 | 33.3 : 66.7 | 31.4 | 32.2 | 28.2 |
| VI | 34.4 : 65.6 | 29.5 : 70.5 | 45.5 : 54.5 | 52.1 : 47.9 | 51.7 : 48.3 | 53.3 : 46.7 | 56.3 : 43.7 | 56.2 : 43.8 | 56.7 : 43.3 | 32.7 | 32.3 | 28.2 |
| VII | 31.5 : 68.5 | 25.2 : 74.8 | 47.5 : 52.5 | 47.8 : 52.2 | 46.9 : 53.1 | 51.4 : 48.6 | 48.8 : 51.2 | 47.5 : 52.5 | 55.1 : 44.9 | 33.2 | 34.1 | 33.9 |
| VIII | 35.8 : 64.2 | 27.7 : 72.3 | 56.8 : 43.2 | 47.3 : 52.7 | 47.5 : 52.5 | 46.2 : 53.8 | 45.2 : 54.8 | 45.7 : 54.3 | 42.5 : 57.5 | 34.6 | 34.8 | 29.6 |
| IX | 34.1 : 65.9 | 25.0 : 75.0 | 61.3 : 38.7 | 51.0 : 49.0 | 51.5 : 48.5 | 51.1 : 48.9 | 51.9 : 48.1 | 52.7 : 47.3 | 47.4 : 52.6 | 33.4 | 33.9 | 34.3 |
| X | 32.0 : 68.0 | 27.8 : 72.2 | 43.5 : 56.5 | 45.9 : 54.1 | 47.0 : 53.0 | 38.4 : 61.6 | 45.8 : 54.2 | 48.3 : 51.6 | 32.8 : 67.2 | 33.3 | 33.6 | 34.6 |
| XI | 34.3 : 65.7 | 27.0 : 73.0 | 51.6 : 48.4 | 48.5 : 51.5 | 51.9 : 48.1 | 36.7 : 63.3 | 50.6 : 49.4 | 52.4 : 47.6 | 42.0 : 58.0 | 32.4 | 33.2 | 32.2 |
| XII | 35.0 : 65.0 | 29.4 : 70.6 | 47.8 : 52.2 | 44.5 : 55.5 | 45.0 : 55.0 | 43.2 : 56.8 | 59.1 : 40.9 | 43.5 : 56.5 | 37.9 : 62.1 | 38.3 | 39.0 | 29.4 |
| | 34.2 : 65.8 | 27.4 : 72.6 | 49.7 : 50.3 | 48.4 : 51.6 | 49.0 : 51.0 | 46.1 : 53.9 | 49.0 : 51.0 | 50.1 : 49.9 | 43.6 : 56.4 | 34.4 | 33.8 | 31.5 |
| *PR* I | 41.9 : 58.1 | 33.2 : 66.8 | 63.8 : 36.2 | 41.8 : 58.2 | 41.2 : 58.8 | 44.2 : 55.8 | 42.3 : 57.7 | 42.2 : 57.8 | 47.6 : 52.4 | 37.2 | 45.1 | 27.1 |
| II | 45.2 : 54.8 | 37.1 : 62.8 | 66.9 : 33.1 | 46.0 : 54.0 | 47.9 : 52.1 | 38.8 : 61.2 | 53.8 : 46.2 | 56.6 : 43.4 | 33.3 : 66.7 | 33.4 | 33.1 | 35.1 |
| III | 43.5 : 56.5 | 34.2 : 65.8 | 66.1 : 33.9 | 42.5 : 57.5 | 42.2 : 57.8 | 42.0 : 58.0 | 43.8 : 56.2 | 43.5 : 56.5 | 45.5 : 54.5 | 42.4 | 43.2 | 38.6 |
| IV | 43.7 : 56.3 | 37.3 : 62.7 | 64.6 : 35.4 | 46.5 : 53.5 | 45.0 : 55.0 | 54.8 : 45.2 | 46.6 : 53.4 | 45.2 : 54.8 | 57.9 : 42.1 | 36.3 | 36.4 | 36.0 |
| | 43.6 : 56.4 | 35.7 : 64.3 | 65.3 : 34.7 | 44.4 : 55.6 | 44.1 : 55.9 | 45.5 : 54.5 | 46.4 : 53.6 | 46.3 : 53.7 | 46.2 : 53.8 | 38.6 | 37.8 | 34.3 |
| *SA* (A) | 42.7 : 57.3 | 37.0 : 63.0 | 56.8 : 43.2 | 45.1 : 54.9 | 47.7 : 52.9 | 36.1 : 63.9 | 42.7 : 57.3 | 47.6 : 52.4 | 22.5 : 77.5 | 37.8 | 37.9 | 37.8 |
| (B) | 45.5 : 54.5 | 32.6 : 67.4 | 75.3 : 24.7 | 47.5 : 52.5 | 48.0 : 52.0 | 43.6 : 56.4 | 45.7 : 54.3 | 49.2 : 50.8 | 14.3 : 85.7 | 36.9 | 36.4 | 40.0 |
| (C) | 50.8 : 49.2 | 34.3 : 65.7 | 78.2 : 21.8 | 51.0 : 49.0 | 50.6 : 49.4 | 52.9 : 47.1 | 51.0 : 49.0 | 49.4 : 50.6 | 61.5 : 38.5 | 32.1 | 32.1 | 32.5 |
| | 45.9 : 54.1 | 34.7 : 65.3 | 69.5 : 30.5 | 47.4 : 52.6 | 48.6 : 51.4 | 42.1 : 57.9 | 45.8 : 54.2 | 48.6 : 51.4 | 29.3 : 70.7 | 36.1 | 35.9 | 37.1 |

## XII. PAUSES

| | Final : internal | | | a : b | | | $e^1 : e^2$ | | | % of odd positions | | |
|---|---|---|---|---|---|---|---|---|---|---|---|---|
| | All punct. marks | Commas | Heavy punct. marks | All punct. marks | Commas | Heavy punct. marks | All punct. marks | Commas | Heavy punct. marks | All punct. marks | Commas | Heavy punct. marks |
| *PL* I-II | 30.9 : 69.1 | 27.4 : 72.6 | 38.8 : 61.2 | 45.9 : 54.1 | 45.3 : 54.7 | 47.8 : 52.2 | 44.5 : 55.5 | 45.6 : 54.4 | 38.3 : 61.7 | 35.1 | 35.3 | 33.2 |
| III-IV | 37.3 : 62.7 | 29.8 : 70.2 | 56.7 : 43.3 | 51.4 : 48.6 | 51.8 : 48.2 | 50.0 : 50.0 | 54.5 : 45.5 | 55.1 : 44.9 | 49.1 : 50.9 | 30.8 | 32.1 | 25.5 |
| V-VI | 32.6 : 67.4 | 26.7 : 73.3 | 47.7 : 52.3 | 49.0 : 51.0 | 49.4 : 50.6 | 47.7 : 52.3 | 52.0 : 48.0 | 52.9 : 47.1 | 47.5 : 52.5 | 32.0 | 32.3 | 31.2 |
| VII-VIII | 33.7 : 66.3 | 26.5 : 73.5 | 52.4 : 47.6 | 47.4 : 52.6 | 47.2 : 52.8 | 49.0 : 51.0 | 47.1 : 52.9 | 46.6 : 53.4 | 49.4 : 50.6 | 33.9 | 34.4 | 31.8 |
| IX-X | 33.1 : 66.9 | 26.3 : 73.7 | 53.0 : 47.0 | 48.6 : 51.4 | 49.6 : 50.4 | 44.0 : 56.0 | 48.4 : 51.6 | 50.8 : 49.2 | 39.7 : 60.3 | 33.4 | 33.8 | 33.2 |
| XI-XII | 34.5 : 65.5 | 27.9 : 72.1 | 50.1 : 49.9 | 47.0 : 53.0 | 49.2 : 50.4 | 39.1 : 60.9 | 47.5 : 52.5 | 48.9 : 51.1 | 40.5 : 59.5 | 34.7 | 35.5 | 32.3 |
| *PL* (Gilbert's Rearrangement) | | | | | | | | | | | | |
| I | 34.6 : 65.4 | 29.4 : 70.6 | 46.7 : 53.3 | 48.8 : 51.2 | 50.1 : 49.9 | 41.2 : 58.8 | 48.1 : 51.9 | 50.0 : 50.0 | 38.9 : 61.1 | 33.0 | 33.9 | 30.0 |
| II | 36.1 : 63.9 | 31.1 : 68.9 | 47.6 : 52.4 | 48.6 : 51.4 | 51.4 : 48.6 | 39.5 : 60.5 | 51.0 : 49.0 | 51.1 : 48.9 | 50.0 : 50.0 | 32.9 | 31.3 | 38.0 |
| III | 33.3 : 66.7 | 27.2 : 72.8 | 53.2 : 46.8 | 49.5 : 50.5 | 49.7 : 50.3 | 47.9 : 52.1 | 47.9 : 52.1 | 49.8 : 50.2 | 29.6 : 70.4 | 31.3 | 32.3 | 26.4 |
| IV | 33.6 : 66.4 | 26.0 : 74.0 | 53.1 : 46.9 | 50.0 : 50.0 | 50.1 : 49.9 | 49.6 : 50.4 | 50.5 : 49.5 | 50.7 : 49.3 | 48.7 : 51.3 | 33.3 | 33.4 | 32.7 |
| V | 33.4 : 66.6 | 26.6 : 73.4 | 50.8 : 49.2 | 45.5 : 54.5 | 45.6 : 54.4 | 45.8 : 54.2 | 49.7 : 50.3 | 48.6 : 51.4 | 37.4 : 62.6 | 32.9 | 33.8 | 29.8 |
| VI | 32.9 : 67.1 | 27.5 : 72.5 | 46.9 : 53.9 | 48.5 : 51.5 | 49.1 : 50.9 | 47.6 : 52.4 | 49.7 : 50.3 | 50.0 : 50.0 | 48.1 : 51.9 | 34.5 | 35.0 | 32.4 |

## XIII. WORD LENGTH

| | No. Words | | | | No. Sylls. | | | | Sylls. per 100 Lines | | | | Positions in rel. to each other | | | |
|---|---|---|---|---|---|---|---|---|---|---|---|---|---|---|---|---|
| | I | II | M | Total | I | II | M | Total | I | II | M | Total | I | II | M | I : II |
| *Comus* | | | | | | | | | | | | | | | | |
| Dis. | 520 | 541 | 117 | 1178 | 1040 | 1082 | 234 | 2356 | 131.3 | 136.6 | 29.6 | 297.5 | 44.1 : 46.0 : 9.9 | | | 49.8 : 50.2 |
| Tris. | 75 | 143 | 37 | 255 | 225 | 429 | 111 | 765 | 28.4 | 54.2 | 14.0 | 96.6 | 29.4 : 56.1 : 14.5 | | | 34.4 : 65.6 |
| Tetr. | 5 | 33 | 9 | 47 | 20 | 132 | 36 | 188 | 2.5 | 19.2 | 5.8 | 27.5 | 9.2 : 69.7 : 21.1 | | | 11.9 : 88.1 } 29.7 : 70.3 |
| Pent. | — | 4 | 2 | 6 | — | 20 | 10 | 30 | | | | | | | | |
| Hex. | — | — | — | — | — | — | — | — | | | | | | | | |
| | | | | | 1285 | 1663 | 391 | 3339 | 162.2 | 210.0 | 49.4 | 421.6 | 38.5 : 49.8 : 11.7 | | | 43.2 : 56.8 |
| *PL* I | | | | | | | | | | | | | | | | |
| Dis. | 603 | 564 | 48 | 1215 | 1206 | 1128 | 96 | 2430 | 151.1 | 141.4 | 12.0 | 304.5 | 49.6 : 46.4 : 4.0 | | | 51.7 : 48.3 |
| Tris. | 144 | 100 | 72 | 316 | 432 | 300 | 216 | 948 | 54.1 | 37.6 | 27.1 | 118.8 | 45.6 : 31.6 : 22.8 | | | 59.0 : 41.0 |
| Tetr. | 17 | 12 | 13 | 42 | 68 | 48 | 52 | 168 | 11.1 | 6.0 | 7.8 | 24.9 | 44.7 : 24.1 : 31.2 | | | 65.0 : 35.0 } 60.0 : 40.0 |
| Pent. | 3 | — | 2 | 5 | 15 | — | 10 | 25 | | | | | | | | |
| Hex. | 1 | — | — | 1 | 6 | — | — | 6 | | | | | | | | |
| | | | | | 1727 | 1476 | 374 | 3577 | 216.4 | 185.0 | 46.9 | 448.3 | 48.3 : 41.3 : 10.4 | | | 53.9 : 46.1 |
| *PL* II | | | | | | | | | | | | | | | | |
| Dis. | 734 | 727 | 82 | 1543 | 1468 | 1454 | 164 | 3086 | 139.1 | 137.8 | 15.6 | 292.5 | 47.6 : 47.1 : 5.3 | | | 50.2 : 49.8 |
| Tris. | 164 | 132 | 69 | 365 | 492 | 396 | 207 | 1095 | 46.6 | 37.5 | 19.6 | 103.7 | 44.9 : 36.2 : 18.9 | | | 55.4 : 44.6 |
| Tetr. | 28 | 17 | 35 | 80 | 112 | 68 | 140 | 320 | 12.5 | 6.9 | 16.3 | 35.7 | 35.0 : 19.4 : 45.6 | | | 64.4 : 35.6 } 57.1 : 42.9 |
| Pent. | 4 | 1 | 4 | 9 | 20 | 5 | 20 | 45 | | | | | | | | |
| Hex. | — | — | 2 | 2 | — | — | 12 | 12 | | | | | | | | |
| | | | | | 2092 | 1923 | 543 | 4558 | 198.3 | 182.3 | 51.5 | 432.0 | 45.9 : 42.2 : 11.9 | | | 52.1 : 47.9 |
| *PL* III | | | | | | | | | | | | | | | | |
| Dis. | 457 | 524 | 70 | 1051 | 914 | 1048 | 140 | 2102 | 123.2 | 141.2 | 18.9 | 283.3 | 43.5 : 49.9 : 6.6 | | | 46.6 : 53.4 |
| Tris. | 128 | 87 | 60 | 275 | 384 | 261 | 180 | 825 | 51.8 | 35.2 | 24.2 | 111.2 | 46.5 : 31.6 : 21.8 | | | 59.5 : 40.5 |
| Tetr. | 24 | 16 | 25 | 65 | 96 | 64 | 100 | 260 | 13.6 | 8.6 | 16.2 | 38.4 | 35.4 : 22.5 : 42.1 | | | 61.2 : 38.8 } 59.9 : 40.1 |
| Pent. | 1 | — | 4 | 5 | 5 | — | 20 | 25 | | | | | | | | |
| Hex. | — | — | — | — | — | — | — | — | | | | | | | | |
| | | | | | 1399 | 1373 | 440 | 3212 | 188.5 | 185.0 | 59.3 | 432.8 | 43.6 : 42.7 : 13.7 | | | 50.5 : 49.5 |

## XIII. WORD LENGTH (Continued)

|  | No. Words ||||  | No. Sylls. ||||  | Sylls. per 100 Lines ||||  | Positions in rel. to each other ||||
|---|---|---|---|---|---|---|---|---|---|---|---|---|---|---|---|---|---|---|---|
|  | I | II | M | Total |  | I | II | M | Total |  | I | II | M | Total |  | I | II | M | I : II |
| *Pl* IV |  |  |  |  |  |  |  |  |  |  |  |  |  |  |  |  |  |  |  |
| Dis. | 691 | 698 | 110 | 1499 |  | 1382 | 1396 | 220 | 2998 |  | 136.2 | 137.5 | 21.7 | 295.4 |  | 46.1 | 46.6 | 7.3 | 49.8 : 50.2 |
| Tris. | 145 | 120 | 86 | 351 |  | 435 | 360 | 258 | 1053 |  | 42.8 | 35.5 | 25.4 | 103.7 |  | 41.3 | 34.2 | 24.5 | 54.7 : 45.3 } 57.6 : 42.4 |
| Tetr. | 25 | 10 | 16 | 51 |  | 100 | 40 | 64 | 204 |  |  |  |  |  |  |  |  |  |  |
| Pent. | 3 | 1 | 1 | 5 |  | 15 | 5 | 5 | 25 |  | 11.2 | 4.4 | 7.4 | 23.1 |  | 48.9 | 19.1 | 31.9 | 71.9 : 28.1 |
| Hex. | — | — | 1 | 1 |  | — | — | 6 | 6 |  |  |  |  |  |  |  |  |  |  |
|  | 1932 |  |  |  |  | 1801 |  | 553 | 4286 |  | 190.3 | 177.4 | 54.5 | 422.3 |  | 45.1 | 42.0 | 12.9 | 51.8 : 48.2 |
| *Pl* V |  |  |  |  |  |  |  |  |  |  |  |  |  |  |  |  |  |  |  |
| Dis. | 554 | 646 | 81 | 1281 |  | 1108 | 1292 | 162 | 2562 |  | 122.6 | 142.9 | 17.9 | 283.4 |  | 43.2 | 50.4 | 6.3 | 46.2 : 53.8 |
| Tris. | 156 | 116 | 75 | 347 |  | 468 | 348 | 225 | 1041 |  | 51.8 | 38.5 | 24.9 | 115.2 |  | 44.9 | 33.5 | 21.6 | 57.3 : 42.7 } 58.9 : 41.1 |
| Tetr. | 24 | 15 | 31 | 70 |  | 96 | 60 | 124 | 280 |  |  |  |  |  |  |  |  |  |  |
| Pent. | 4 | — | 5 | 9 |  | 20 | — | 25 | 45 |  | 12.8 | 6.6 | 16.5 | 35.9 |  | 35.7 | 18.5 | 45.8 | 65.9 : 34.1 |
| Hex. | — | — | — | — |  | — | — | — | — |  |  |  |  |  |  |  |  |  |  |
|  | 1692 |  |  |  |  | 1700 |  | 536 | 3928 |  | 187.2 | 188.1 | 59.3 | 434.5 |  | 43.1 | 43.3 | 13.6 | 49.9 : 50.1 |
| *Pl* VI |  |  |  |  |  |  |  |  |  |  |  |  |  |  |  |  |  |  |  |
| Dis. | 614 | 604 | 133 | 1351 |  | 1228 | 1208 | 266 | 2702 |  | 134.6 | 132.5 | 29.2 | 296.3 |  | 45.5 | 44.6 | 9.8 | 50.4 : 49.6 |
| Tris. | 153 | 108 | 116 | 377 |  | 459 | 324 | 348 | 1131 |  | 50.3 | 35.5 | 38.2 | 124.0 |  | 40.6 | 28.6 | 30.8 | 58.6 : 41.4 } 62.7 : 37.3 |
| Tetr. | 33 | 8 | 24 | 65 |  | 132 | 32 | 96 | 260 |  |  |  |  |  |  |  |  |  |  |
| Pent. | 3 | 1 | 12 | 16 |  | 15 | 5 | 60 | 80 |  | 16.1 | 4.1 | 17.1 | 37.3 |  | 43.2 | 10.9 | 45.9 | 79.9 : 20.1 |
| Hex. | — | — | — | — |  | — | — | — | — |  |  |  |  |  |  |  |  |  |  |
|  | 1834 |  |  |  |  | 1569 |  | 770 | 4173 |  | 201.0 | 172.0 | 84.4 | 457.5 |  | 43.9 | 37.6 | 18.5 | 53.9 : 46.1 |
| *Pl* VII |  |  |  |  |  |  |  |  |  |  |  |  |  |  |  |  |  |  |  |
| Dis. | 427 | 418 | 68 | 913 |  | 854 | 836 | 136 | 1826 |  | 133.4 | 130.6 | 21.3 | 285.3 |  | 46.8 | 45.8 | 7.4 | 50.5 : 49.5 |
| Tris. | 119 | 76 | 58 | 253 |  | 357 | 228 | 174 | 759 |  | 55.8 | 35.6 | 27.2 | 118.6 |  | 47.0 | 30.0 | 22.9 | 61.0 : 39.0 } 61.5 : 38.5 |
| Tetr. | 21 | 12 | 24 | 57 |  | 84 | 48 | 96 | 228 |  |  |  |  |  |  |  |  |  |  |
| Pent. | — | — | 5 | 5 |  | — | — | 25 | 25 |  | 13.1 | 7.5 | 18.9 | 39.5 |  | 33.2 | 19.0 | 47.8 | 63.6 : 36.4 |
| Hex. | — | — | — | — |  | — | — | — | — |  |  |  |  |  |  |  |  |  |  |
|  | 1295 |  |  |  |  | 1112 |  | 431 | 2838 |  | 202.3 | 173.8 | 67.3 | 443.4 |  | 45.6 | 39.2 | 15.2 | 53.8 : 46.2 |

XIII. WORD LENGTH (Continued)

| | No. Words | | | | No. Sylls. | | | | Sylls. per 100 Lines | | | | Positions in rel. to each other | | |
|---|---|---|---|---|---|---|---|---|---|---|---|---|---|---|---|
| | I | II | M | Total | I | II | M | Total | I | II | M | Total | I | II | M | I : II |
| *PL* VIII | | | | | | | | | | | | | | | | |
| Dis. | 391 | 400 | 42 | 833 | 782 | 800 | 84 | 1666 | 120.6 | 123.3 | 13.0 | 256.9 | 46.9 : 48.0 : 5.0 | | | 49.4 : 50.6 |
| Tris. | 152 | 100 | 72 | 324 | 456 | 300 | 216 | 972 | 70.3 | 46.2 | 33.3 | 149.8 | 46.9 : 30.9 : 22.2 | | | 60.3 : 39.7 |
| Tetr. | 15 | 10 | 32 | 57 | 60 | 40 | 128 | 228 | | | 22.2 | 41.6 | 25.9 : 20.7 : 53.3 | | | 55.5 : 44.5 | 59.6 : 40.4 |
| Pent. | 2 | 2 | 2 | 6 | 10 | 10 | 10 | 30 | 10.8 | 8.6 | | | | | | |
| Hex. | — | 1 | 1 | 2 | — | 6 | 6 | 12 | | | | | | | | |
| | 1308 | | | | | 1156 | 444 | 2908 | 201.6 | 178.1 | 68.4 | 448.1 | 45.0 : 39.7 : 15.3 | | | 53.1 : 46.9 |
| *PL* IX | | | | | | | | | | | | | | | | |
| Dis. | 777 | 816 | 111 | 1704 | 1554 | 1632 | 222 | 3408 | 130.7 | 137.3 | 18.7 | 286.7 | 45.6 : 47.9 : 6.5 | | | 48.8 : 51.2 |
| Tris. | 177 | 141 | 118 | 436 | 531 | 423 | 354 | 1308 | 44.7 | 35.6 | 29.8 | 110.1 | 40.6 : 32.3 : 27.1 | | | 55.7 : 44.3 |
| Tetr. | 27 | 16 | 22 | 65 | 108 | 64 | 88 | 260 | | | 11.3 | 26.4 | 35.7 : 21.8 : 42.4 | | | 62.1 : 37.9 | 55.8 : 44.2 |
| Pent. | 1 | 1 | 8 | 10 | 5 | 5 | 40 | 50 | 9.4 | 5.8 | | | | | | |
| Hex. | — | — | 1 | 1 | — | — | 6 | 6 | | | | | | | | |
| | | | | | 2198 | 2124 | 710 | 5032 | 184.9 | 178.6 | 59.7 | 423.2 | 43.7 : 42.2 : 14.1 | | | 50.9 : 49.1 |
| *PL* X | | | | | | | | | | | | | | | | |
| Dis. | 661 | 702 | 120 | 1483 | 1322 | 1404 | 240 | 2966 | 119.8 | 127.2 | 21.7 | 268.7 | 44.6 : 47.3 : 8.1 | | | 48.5 : 51.5 |
| Tris. | 202 | 151 | 119 | 472 | 606 | 453 | 357 | 1416 | 54.9 | 41.0 | 32.3 | 128.2 | 42.8 : 32.0 : 25.2 | | | 57.2 : 42.8 |
| Tetr. | 38 | 27 | 29 | 94 | 152 | 108 | 116 | 376 | | | 13.7 | 40.0 | 37.8 : 28.0 : 34.2 | | | 57.4 : 42.6 | 57.3 : 42.7 |
| Pent. | 3 | 2 | 7 | 12 | 15 | 10 | 35 | 60 | 15.1 | 11.2 | | | | | | |
| Hex. | — | 1 | — | 1 | — | 6 | — | 6 | | | | | | | | |
| | | | | | 2095 | 1981 | 748 | 4824 | 189.8 | 179.45 | 67.75 | 437.0 | 43.4 : 41.1 : 15.5 | | | 51.4 : 48.6 |
| *PL* XI | | | | | | | | | | | | | | | | |
| Dis. | 554 | 627 | 94 | 1275 | 1108 | 1254 | 188 | 2550 | 123.6 | 139.8 | 20.9 | 284.3 | 43.4 : 49.2 : 7.4 | | | 46.9 : 53.1 |
| Tris. | 151 | 102 | 64 | 317 | 453 | 306 | 192 | 951 | 50.5 | 34.1 | 21.4 | 106.0 | 47.6 : 32.2 : 20.2 | | | 59.7 : 40.3 |
| Tetr. | 16 | 13 | 22 | 51 | 64 | 52 | 88 | 204 | | | 10.9 | 25.0 | 33.0 : 23.2 : 43.8 | | | 58.7 : 41.3 | 59.6 : 40.4 |
| Pent. | 2 | — | 2 | 4 | 10 | — | 10 | 20 | 8.3 | 5.8 | | | | | | |
| Hex. | — | — | — | — | — | — | — | — | | | | | | | | |
| | | | | | 1635 | 1612 | 478 | 3725 | 182.3 | 179.7 | 53.3 | 415.3 | 43.9 : 43.3 : 12.8 | | | 50.4 : 49.6 |

## XIII. WORD LENGTH (Continued)

| | No. Words | | | | No. Sylls. | | | | Sylls. per 100 Lines | | | | Positions in rel. to each other | | | |
|---|---|---|---|---|---|---|---|---|---|---|---|---|---|---|---|---|
| | I | II | M | Total | I | II | M | Total | I | II | M | Total | I | II | M | I : II | |
| *PL XII* | | | | | | | | | | | | | | | | | |
| Dis. | 424 | 440 | 63 | 927 | 848 | 880 | 126 | 1854 | 131.7 | 136.6 | 19.6 | 287.9 | 45.7 | 47.5 | 6.8 | 49.1 : 50.9 | |
| Tris. | 94 | 83 | 58 | 235 | 282 | 249 | 174 | 705 | 44.1 | 39.0 | 27.2 | 110.3 | 40.0 | 35.3 | 24.7 | 53.1 : 46.9 | 55.2 : 44.8 |
| Tetr. | 14 | 7 | 20 | 41 | 56 | 28 | 80 | 164 | | | 12.4 | | | | | | |
| Pent. | 3 | 2 | — | 5 | 15 | 10 | — | 25 | 11.0 | 5.9 | | 29.3 | 37.6 | 20.1 | 42.3 | 65.1 : 34.9 | |
| Hex. | — | — | — | — | — | — | — | — | | | | | | | | | |
| | 1201 | 1167 | 380 | 2748 | | | | | 186.5 | 181.2 | 59.0 | 426.7 | 43.7 : 42.5 : 13.8 | | | 50.7 : 49.3 | |
| *PL I-XII* | | | | | | | | | | | | | | | | | |
| Dis. | 6887 | 7166 | 1022 | 15075 | 13774 | 14332 | 2044 | 30150 | 130.6 | 135.8 | 19.4 | 285.8 | 45.7 | 47.5 | 6.8 | 49.0 : 51.0 | |
| Tris. | 1785 | 1316 | 967 | 4068 | 5355 | 3948 | 2901 | 12204 | 50.6 | 37.5 | 27.5 | 115.7 | 43.9 | 32.4 | 23.7 | 57.6 : 42.4 | 58.7 : 41.3 |
| Tetr. | 282 | 163 | 293 | 738 | 1128 | 652 | 1172 | 2952 | 12.1 | 6.7 | 13.9 | 32.7 | | | | | |
| Pent. | 29 | 10 | 52 | 91 | 145 | 50 | 260 | 455 | | | | | 37.0 | 20.7 | 42.3 | 64.2 : 35.8 | |
| Hex. | 1 | 2 | 5 | 8 | 6 | 12 | 30 | 48 | | | | | | | | | |
| | 20408 | 18994 | 6407 | 45809 | | | | | 193.4 | 180.1 | 60.7 | 434.2 | 44.6 : 41.5 : 13.9 | | | 51.8 : 48.2 | |
| *PR I* | | | | | | | | | | | | | | | | | |
| Dis. | 316 | 342 | 55 | 713 | 632 | 684 | 110 | 1426 | 125.9 | 136.3 | 21.9 | 284.1 | 44.3 | 48.0 | 7.7 | 48.0 : 52.0 | |
| Tris. | 72 | 63 | 44 | 179 | 216 | 189 | 132 | 537 | 43.0 | 37.6 | 26.3 | 106.9 | 40.2 | 35.2 | 24.6 | 53.3 : 46.7 | 54.9 : 45.1 |
| Tetr. | 10 | 4 | 12 | 26 | 40 | 16 | 48 | 104 | 8.0 | 4.2 | 11.5 | 23.7 | | | | | |
| Pent. | — | 1 | 2 | 3 | — | 5 | 10 | 15 | | | | | 33.6 | 17.6 | 48.7 | 65.6 : 34.4 | |
| Hex. | — | — | — | — | — | — | — | — | | | | | | | | | |
| | 888 | 894 | 300 | 2082 | | | | | 176.9 | 178.1 | 59.8 | 414.7 | 42.7 : 42.9 : 14.4 | | | 49.3 : 50.7 | |
| *PR II* | | | | | | | | | | | | | | | | | |
| Dis. | 358 | 336 | 48 | 742 | 716 | 672 | 96 | 1484 | 147.3 | 138.3 | 19.7 | 305.3 | 48.2 | 45.3 | 6.5 | 51.6 : 48.4 | |
| Tris. | 52 | 73 | 47 | 172 | 156 | 219 | 141 | 516 | 32.1 | 45.1 | 29.0 | 106.2 | 30.2 | 42.4 | 27.3 | 41.6 : 58.4 | 42.8 : 57.2 |
| Tetr. | 8 | 8 | 15 | 31 | 32 | 32 | 60 | 124 | 6.6 | 6.6 | 12.3 | 25.5 | | | | | |
| Pent. | — | — | — | — | — | — | — | — | | | | | 25.8 | 25.8 | 48.4 | 50.0 : 50.0 | |
| Hex. | — | — | — | — | — | — | — | — | | | | | | | | | |
| | 904 | 923 | 297 | 2124 | | | | | 186.0 | 189.9 | 61.1 | 437.0 | 42.6 : 43.4 : 14.0 | | | 49.5 : 50.5 | |

## XIII. WORD LENGTH (Continued)

| | No. Words | | | | No. Sylls. | | | | Sylls. per 100 Lines | | | | Positions in rel. to each other | | | |
|---|---|---|---|---|---|---|---|---|---|---|---|---|---|---|---|---|
| | I | II | M | Total | I | II | M | Total | I | II | M | Total | I | II | M | I : II |
| **PR III** | | | | | | | | | | | | | | | | |
| Dis. | 282 | 299 | 58 | 639 | 564 | 598 | 116 | 1278 | 127.3 | 135.0 | 26.2 | 288.5 | 44.1 : 46.8 : 9.1 | | | 48.5 : 51.5 |
| Tris. | 52 | 78 | 33 | 163 | 156 | 234 | 99 | 489 | 35.2 | 52.8 | 22.3 | 110.3 | 31.9 : 47.9 : 20.2 | | | 40.0 : 60.0 |
| Tetr. | 25 | 15 | 13 | 53 | 100 | 60 | 52 | 212 | 24.8 | 13.5 | 17.4 | 55.7 | 44.5 : 24.3 : 31.2 | | | 64.7 : 35.3 } 47.5 : 52.5 |
| Pent. | 2 | — | 5 | 7 | 10 | — | 25 | 35 | | | | | | | | |
| Hex. | — | — | — | — | — | — | — | — | | | | | | | | |
| | | | | | 830 | 892 | 292 | 2014 | 187.4 | 201.3 | 65.9 | 454.6 | 41.2 : 44.3 : 14.5 | | | 48.2 : 51.8 |
| **PR IV** | | | | | | | | | | | | | | | | |
| Dis. | 434 | 436 | 47 | 917 | 868 | 872 | 94 | 1834 | 135.8 | 136.5 | 14.7 | 287.0 | 47.3 : 47.5 : 5.1 | | | 49.9 : 50.1 |
| Tris. | 90 | 96 | 58 | 244 | 270 | 288 | 174 | 732 | 42.3 | 45.1 | 27.2 | 114.6 | 36.9 : 39.3 : 23.8 | | | 48.4 : 51.6 |
| Tetr. | 11 | 17 | 9 | 37 | 44 | 68 | 36 | 148 | 8.5 | 10.6 | 8.8 | 27.9 | 30.3 : 38.2 : 31.5 | | | 44.3 : 55.7 } 47.6 : 52.4 |
| Pent. | 2 | — | 4 | 6 | 10 | — | 20 | 30 | | | | | | | | |
| Hex. | — | — | — | — | — | — | — | — | | | | | | | | |
| | | | | | 1192 | 1228 | 324 | 2744 | 186.5 | 192.2 | 50.7 | 429.4 | 43.4 : 44.8 : 11.8 | | | 49.2 : 50.8 |
| **PR I-IV** | | | | | | | | | | | | | | | | |
| Dis. | 1390 | 1413 | 208 | 3011 | 2780 | 2826 | 416 | 6022 | 134.3 | 136.5 | 20.1 | 290.9 | 46.2 : 46.9 : 6.9 | | | 49.6 : 50.4 |
| Tris. | 266 | 310 | 182 | 758 | 798 | 930 | 546 | 2274 | 38.6 | 44.9 | 26.4 | 109.9 | 35.1 : 40.9 : 24.0 | | | 46.2 : 53.8 |
| Tetr. | 54 | 44 | 49 | 147 | 216 | 176 | 196 | 588 | 11.4 | 9.0 | 12.1 | 32.6 | 35.0 : 27.7 : 37.2 | | | 56.6 : 43.4 } 48.2 : 51.8 |
| Pent. | 4 | 1 | 11 | 16 | 20 | 5 | 55 | 80 | | | | | | | | |
| Hex. | — | — | — | — | — | — | — | — | | | | | | | | |
| | | | | | 3814 | 3937 | 1213 | 8964 | 184.3 | 190.4 | 58.6 | 433.4 | 42.4 : 43.9 : 13.5 | | | 49.0 : 51.0 |
| **SA (A)** | | | | | | | | | | | | | | | | |
| Dis. | 310 | 334 | 57 | 701 | 620 | 668 | 114 | 1402 | 130.8 | 141.0 | 24.0 | 295.8 | 44.2 : 47.6 : 8.1 | | | 48.1 : 51.9 |
| Tris. | 80 | 71 | 36 | 187 | 240 | 213 | 108 | 561 | 50.6 | 44.9 | 22.8 | 118.3 | 42.8 : 38.0 : 19.2 | | | 53.0 : 47.0 |
| Tetr. | 12 | 8 | 15 | 35 | 48 | 32 | 60 | 140 | 13.3 | 6.7 | 16.9 | 36.9 | 36.0 : 18.3 : 45.7 | | | 66.3 : 33.7 } 55.3 : 44.7 |
| Pent. | 3 | — | 4 | 7 | 15 | — | 20 | 35 | | | | | | | | |
| Hex. | — | — | — | — | — | — | — | — | | | | | | | | |
| | | | | | 923 | 913 | 302 | 2138 | 194.7 | 192.6 | 63.7 | 451.0 | 43.2 : 42.7 : 14.1 | | | 50.3 : 49.7 |

## XIII. WORD LENGTH (*Continued*)

| | No. Words | | | | No. Sylls. | | | | Sylls. per 100 Lines | | | | Positions in rel. to each other | | | |
|---|---|---|---|---|---|---|---|---|---|---|---|---|---|---|---|---|
| | I | II | M | Total | I | II | M | Total | I | II | M | Total | I | II | M | I : II | |
| *SA* (B) | | | | | | | | | | | | | | | | | |
| Dis. | 280 | 343 | 63 | 686 | 560 | 686 | 126 | 1372 | 113.8 | 139.4 | 25.6 | 278.8 | 40.8 : 50.0 : 9.2 | | | 44.9 : 55.1 | |
| Tris. | 76 | 78 | 51 | 205 | 228 | 234 | 153 | 615 | 46.3 | 47.6 | 31.1 | 125.0 | 37.1 : 38.0 : 24.9 | | | 49.4 : 50.6 | 50.1 : 49.9 |
| Tetr. | 12 | 9 | 17 | 38 | 48 | 36 | 68 | 152 | 9.8 | 8.3 | 20.9 | 39.0 | 25.0 : 21.4 : 53.6 | | | 53.9 : 46.1 | |
| Pent. | — | 1 | 7 | 8 | — | 5 | 35 | 40 | | | | | | | | | |
| Hex. | — | — | — | — | — | — | — | — | | | | | | | | | |
| | | | | | 836 | 961 | 382 | 2179 | 169.9 | 195.3 | 77.6 | 442.8 | 38.4 : 44.1 : 17.5 | | | 46.5 : 53.5 | |
| *SA* (C) | | | | | | | | | | | | | | | | | |
| Dis. | 235 | 256 | 52 | 543 | 470 | 512 | 104 | 1086 | 126.3 | 137.6 | 28.0 | 291.9 | 43.3 : 47.1 : 9.6 | | | 47.9 : 52.1 | |
| Tris. | 38 | 58 | 28 | 124 | 114 | 174 | 84 | 372 | 30.7 | 46.8 | 22.5 | 100.0 | 30.6 : 46.8 : 22.6 | | | 39.6 : 60.4 | 38.5 : 61.5 |
| Tetr. | 9 | 14 | 13 | 36 | 36 | 56 | 52 | 144 | 9.7 | 17.7 | 20.7 | 48.1 | 20.1 : 36.9 : 43.0 | | | 35.3 : 64.7 | |
| Pent. | — | 2 | 5 | 7 | — | 10 | 25 | 35 | | | | | | | | | |
| Hex. | — | — | — | — | — | — | — | — | | | | | | | | | |
| | | | | | 620 | 752 | 265 | 1637 | 166.7 | 202.2 | 71.2 | 440.1 | 37.9 : 45.9 : 16.2 | | | 45.2 : 54.8 | |
| *SA* (A-C) | | | | | | | | | | | | | | | | | |
| Dis. | 825 | 933 | 172 | 1930 | 1650 | 1866 | 344 | 3860 | 123.3 | 139.5 | 25.7 | 288.5 | 42.7 : 48.3 : 9.0 | | | 46.9 : 53.1 | |
| Tris. | 194 | 207 | 115 | 516 | 582 | 621 | 345 | 1548 | 43.5 | 46.4 | 25.8 | 115.7 | 37.6 : 40.1 : 22.3 | | | 48.4 : 51.6 | 49.0 : 51.0 |
| Tetr. | 33 | 31 | 45 | 109 | 132 | 124 | 180 | 436 | 11.0 | 10.4 | 19.4 | 40.8 | 26.9 : 25.5 : 47.6 | | | 51.4 : 48.6 | |
| Pent. | 3 | 3 | 16 | 22 | 15 | 15 | 80 | 110 | | | | | | | | | |
| Hex. | — | — | — | — | — | — | — | — | | | | | | | | | |
| | | | | | 2379 | 2626 | 949 | 5954 | 177.8 | 196.3 | 70.9 | 445.0 | 40.0 : 44.1 : 15.9 | | | 47.5 : 52.5 | |

## XIV. WORD LENGTH

| | No. Words | | | | No. Sylls. | | | | Sylls. Per 100 Lines | | | | Position in rel. to each other | | |
|---|---|---|---|---|---|---|---|---|---|---|---|---|---|---|---|
| | I | II | M | Total | I | II | M | Total | I | II | M | Total | I : II : M | I : II : M | I : II |
| *Pl I-II* | | | | | | | | | | | | | | | |
| Dis. | 1337 | 1291 | 130 | 2758 | 2674 | 2582 | 260 | 5516 | 144.3 | 139.4 | 14.0 | 297.7 | 48.5 : 46.8 : 4.7 | 50.9 : 49.1 | |
| Tris. | 308 | 232 | 141 | 681 | 924 | 696 | 423 | 2043 | 49.9 | 37.5 | 22.8 | 110.2 | 45.2 : 34.1 : 20.7 | 57.0 : 43.0 | 58.4 : 41.6 |
| Tetr. | 45 | 29 | 48 | 122 | 180 | 116 | 192 | 488 | | 6.6 | 12.6 | 31.1 | 38.4 : 21.0 : 40.6 | 64.6 : 35.4 | |
| Pent. | 7 | 1 | 6 | 14 | 35 | 5 | 30 | 70 | 11.9 | | | | | | |
| Hex. | 1 | — | 2 | 3 | 6 | — | 12 | 18 | | | | | | | |
| | | | | | 3819 | 3399 | 917 | 8135 | 206.1 | 183.6 | 49.4 | 439.1 | 46.9 : 41.8 : 11.3 | 53.0 : 47.0 | |
| *Pl III-IV* | | | | | | | | | | | | | | | |
| Dis. | 1148 | 1222 | 180 | 2550 | 2296 | 2444 | 360 | 5100 | 129.9 | 138.3 | 20.3 | 288.5 | 45.0 : 47.8 : 7.1 | 48.4 : 51.6 | |
| Tris. | 273 | 207 | 146 | 626 | 819 | 621 | 438 | 1878 | 46.3 | 35.1 | 24.8 | 106.3 | 43.6 : 33.1 : 23.3 | 56.9 : 43.1 | |
| Tetr. | 49 | 26 | 41 | 116 | 196 | 104 | 164 | 464 | 12.2 | 6.2 | 11.0 | 29.4 | 41.5 : 20.9 : 37.5 | 66.0 : 34.0 | 58.7 : 41.3 |
| Pent. | 4 | 1 | 5 | 10 | 20 | 5 | 25 | 50 | | | | | | | |
| Hex. | — | — | 1 | 1 | — | — | 6 | 6 | | | | | | | |
| | | | | | 3331 | 3174 | 993 | 7498 | 188.6 | 179.4 | 56.2 | 424.2 | 44.4 : 42.3 : 13.2 | 51.2 : 48.8 | |
| *Pl V-VI* | | | | | | | | | | | | | | | |
| Dis. | 1168 | 1250 | 214 | 2632 | 2336 | 2500 | 428 | 5264 | 128.6 | 137.6 | 23.6 | 289.8 | 44.4 : 47.5 : 8.1 | 47.9 : 52.1 | |
| Tris. | 309 | 224 | 191 | 724 | 927 | 672 | 573 | 2172 | 51.0 | 37.0 | 31.6 | 119.6 | 42.7 : 30.9 : 26.4 | 58.0 : 42.0 | |
| Tetr. | 57 | 23 | 55 | 135 | 228 | 92 | 220 | 540 | 14.5 | 5.3 | 16.8 | 36.6 | 39.5 : 14.6 : 45.9 | 72.9 : 27.1 | 60.7 : 39.3 |
| Pent. | 7 | 1 | 17 | 25 | 35 | 5 | 85 | 125 | | | | | | | |
| Hex. | — | — | — | — | — | — | — | — | | | | | | | |
| | | | | | 3526 | 3269 | 1306 | 8101 | 194.2 | 180.0 | 71.9 | 446.1 | 43.5 : 40.4 : 16.1 | 51.9 : 48.1 | |
| *Pl VII-VIII* | | | | | | | | | | | | | | | |
| Dis. | 818 | 818 | 110 | 1746 | 1636 | 1636 | 220 | 3492 | 126.9 | 126.9 | 17.1 | 270.9 | 46.8 : 46.8 : 6.4 | 50.0 : 50.0 | |
| Tris. | 271 | 176 | 130 | 577 | 813 | 528 | 390 | 1731 | 63.1 | 40.9 | 31.3 | 134.3 | 47.0 : 30.5 : 22.5 | 60.6 : 39.4 | |
| Tetr. | 36 | 22 | 56 | 114 | 144 | 88 | 224 | 456 | 11.9 | 8.1 | 20.6 | 40.6 | 29.4 : 19.9 : 50.7 | 59.7 : 40.3 | 60.4 : 39.6 |
| Pent. | 2 | 2 | 7 | 11 | 10 | 10 | 35 | 55 | | | | | | | |
| Hex. | — | 1 | 1 | 2 | — | 6 | 6 | 12 | | | | | | | |
| | | | | | 2603 | 2268 | 875 | 5746 | 201.9 | 176.0 | 67.9 | 445.8 | 45.3 : 39.5 : 15.2 | 53.4 : 46.6 | |

## XIV. WORD LENGTH (Continued)

| | No. Words | | | No. Sylls. | | | | Sylls. Per 100 Lines | | | | Position in rel. to each other | |
|---|---|---|---|---|---|---|---|---|---|---|---|---|---|
| | I | II | M | Total | I | II | M | Total | I | II | M | Total | I : II : M | I : II |
| *PL IX-X* | | | | | | | | | | | | | | |
| Dis. | 1438 | 1518 | 231 | 3187 | 2876 | 3036 | 462 | 6374 | 125.4 | 132.4 | 20.1 | 277.9 | 45.1 : 47.6 : 7.3 | 48.6 : 51.4 |
| Tris. | 379 | 292 | 237 | 908 | 1137 | 876 | 711 | 2724 | 49.5 | 37.3 | 31.0 | 118.8 | 41.7 : 32.2 : 26.1 | 56.5 : 43.5 |
| Tetr. | 65 | 43 | 51 | 159 | 260 | 172 | 204 | 636 | 12.2 | 8.4 | 12.4 | 33.0 | 36.9 : 25.5 : 37.6 | 59.2 : 40.8 | 57.0 : 43.0
| Pent. | 4 | 3 | 15 | 22 | 20 | 15 | 75 | 110 | | | | | | |
| Hex. | — | 1 | 1 | 2 | — | 6 | 6 | 12 | | | | | | |
| | | | | | 4293 | 4105 | 1458 | 9856 | 187.2 | 179.0 | 63.6 | 429.8 | 43.6 : 41.6 : 14.8 | 51.1 : 48.9 |
| *PL XI-XII* | | | | | | | | | | | | | | |
| Dis. | 978 | 1067 | 157 | 2202 | 1956 | 2134 | 314 | 4404 | 126.9 | 138.5 | 20.4 | 285.8 | 44.4 : 48.5 : 7.1 | 47.8 : 52.2 |
| Tris. | 245 | 185 | 122 | 552 | 735 | 555 | 366 | 1656 | 47.7 | 36.0 | 23.8 | 107.5 | 44.4 : 33.5 : 22.1 | 57.0 : 43.0 |
| Tetr. | 30 | 20 | 42 | 92 | 120 | 80 | 168 | 368 | 9.4 | 5.8 | 11.6 | 26.8 | 35.1 : 21.8 : 43.1 | 61.7 : 38.3 | 57.7 : 42.3
| Pent. | 5 | 2 | 2 | 9 | 25 | 10 | 10 | 45 | | | | | | |
| Hex. | — | — | — | — | — | — | — | — | | | | | | |
| | | | | | 2836 | 2779 | 858 | 6473 | 184.0 | 180.3 | 55.7 | 420.0 | 43.8 : 42.9 : 13.3 | 50.6 : 49.4 |

## XV. WORD LENGTH IN PL (GILBERT)

| | | No. Words | | | No. Sylls. | | | | Sylls. Per 100 Lines | | | | | | |
|---|---|---|---|---|---|---|---|---|---|---|---|---|---|---|---|
| | | I | II | M | Total | I | II | M | Total | I | II | M | Total | I : II : M | (I) : II | I : II (Polys.) |
| **Group I** | | | | | | | | | | | | | | | | |
| | Dis. | 917 | 1000 | 208 | 2125 | 1834 | 2000 | 416 | 4250 | 118.4 | 129.1 | 26.9 | 274.4 | 43.1 : 47.1 : 9.8 | : 52.2 | |
| | Tris. | 245 | 186 | 121 | 552 | 735 | 558 | 363 | 1656 | 47.5 | 36.0 | 23.9 | 107.4 | 44.4 : 33.7 : 21.9 | : 43.2 | |
| | Tetr. | 43 | 25 | 40 | 108 | 172 | 100 | 160 | 432 | | | | | | | 61.0 : 39.0 |
| | Pent. | 5 | 4 | 5 | 14 | 25 | 20 | 25 | 70 | 12.7 | 8.1 | 12.0 | 32.8 | 38.8 : 24.8 : 36.4 | : 42.3 | |
| | Hex. | — | 1 | — | 1 | — | 6 | — | 6 | | | | | | | |
| | | 2766 | 2684 | 964 | 6414 | | | | | 178.6 | 173.3 | 62.8 | 414.7 | 43.1 : 41.8 : 15.0 | : 49.3 | |
| **Group II** | | | | | | | | | | | | | | | | |
| | Dis. | 324 | 351 | 39 | 714 | 648 | 702 | 78 | 1428 | 132.0 | 143.0 | 15.9 | 290.9 | 45.3 : 49.2 : 5.5 | : 52.0 | |
| | Tris. | 73 | 45 | 34 | 152 | 219 | 135 | 102 | 456 | 44.6 | 27.5 | 20.8 | 92.9 | 48.0 : 29.6 : 22.4 | : 38.1 | |
| | Tetr. | 8 | 8 | 6 | 22 | 32 | 32 | 24 | 88 | | | | | | | 53.6 : 46.4 |
| | Pent. | 1 | — | 1 | 2 | 5 | — | 5 | 10 | 7.6 | 6.5 | 5.9 | 19.9 | 37.7 : 32.7 : 29.6 | : 39.5 | |
| | Hex. | — | — | — | — | — | — | — | — | | | | | | | |
| | | 904 | 869 | 209 | 1982 | | | | | 184.1 | 177.0 | 42.6 | 403.7 | 45.6 : 43.8 : 10.5 | : 49.6 | |
| **Group III** | | | | | | | | | | | | | | | | |
| | Dis. | 566 | 574 | 77 | 1217 | 1132 | 1148 | 154 | 2434 | 138.6 | 140.5 | 18.8 | 297.9 | 46.5 : 47.2 : 6.3 | : 50.4 | |
| | Tris. | 119 | 95 | 82 | 296 | 357 | 285 | 246 | 888 | 43.7 | 34.9 | 30.1 | 108.8 | 40.2 : 32.1 : 27.7 | : 44.4 | |
| | Tetr. | 20 | 13 | 22 | 55 | 80 | 52 | 88 | 220 | | | | | | | 64.8 : 35.2 |
| | Pent. | 5 | 1 | — | 6 | 25 | 5 | — | 30 | 12.9 | 6.9 | 10.8 | 30.6 | 42.0 : 22.8 : 35.2 | : 42.5 | |
| | Hex. | — | — | — | — | — | — | — | — | | | | | | | |
| | | 1594 | 1490 | 488 | 3572 | | | | | 195.2 | 182.4 | 59.7 | 437.3 | 44.6 : 41.7 : 13.7 | : 48.3 | |
| **Group IV** | | | | | | | | | | | | | | | | |
| | Dis. | 1654 | 1637 | 189 | 3480 | 3308 | 3274 | 378 | 6960 | 135.6 | 134.2 | 15.5 | 285.3 | 47.5 : 47.0 : 5.4 | : 49.7 | |
| | Tris. | 436 | 305 | 248 | 989 | 1308 | 915 | 744 | 2967 | 53.6 | 37.5 | 30.5 | 121.6 | 44.1 : 30.8 : 25.1 | : 41.2 | |
| | Tetr. | 62 | 27 | 66 | 155 | 248 | 108 | 264 | 620 | | | | | | | 68.0 : 32.0 |
| | Pent. | 3 | 2 | 21 | 26 | 15 | 10 | 105 | 130 | 10.8 | 5.1 | 15.2 | 30.9 | 34.8 : 16.4 : 48.8 | : 39.8 | |
| | Hex. | — | 1 | — | 1 | — | 6 | — | 6 | | | | | | | |
| | | 4879 | 4313 | 1491 | 10683 | | | | | 200.1 | 176.8 | 61.1 | 438.0 | 45.7 : 40.4 : 13.9 | : 46.9 | |

## XV. WORD LENGTH IN *PL* (GILBERT) *(Continued)*

| | No. Words | | | | No. Sylls. | | | | Sylls. Per 100 Lines | | | | | | |
|---|---|---|---|---|---|---|---|---|---|---|---|---|---|---|---|
| | I | II | M | Total | I | II | M | Total | I | II | M | Total | I : II : M | (I) : II | I : II (Polys.) |
| **Group V** | | | | | | | | | | | | | | | |
| Dis. | 1663 | 1759 | 218 | 3640 | 3326 | 3518 | 436 | 7280 | 133.1 | 140.7 | 17.5 | 291.3 | 45.7 : 48.3 : 6.0 | 51.4 | |
| Tris. | 436 | 320 | 224 | 980 | 1308 | 960 | 672 | 2940 | 52.3 | 38.4 | 26.9 | 117.6 | 44.5 : 32.6 : 22.9 | : 42.5 | 67.7 : 32.3 |
| Tetr. | 66 | 37 | 70 | 173 | 264 | 148 | 280 | 692 | 12.4 | 5.9 | 13.2 | 31.5 | 39.3 : 18.8 : 41.9 | 40.6 | |
| Pent. | 8 | — | 10 | 18 | 40 | — | 50 | 90 | | | | | | | |
| Hex. | 1 | — | — | 1 | 6 | — | — | 6 | | | | | | | |
| | | | | | 4944 | 4626 | 1438 | 11008 | 197.8 | 185.1 | 57.5 | 440.4 | 44.9 : 42.0 : 13.1 | : 48.3 | |
| **Group VI** | | | | | | | | | | | | | | | |
| Dis. | 1763 | 1845 | 291 | 3899 | 3526 | 3690 | 582 | 7798 | 127.3 | 133.3 | 21.0 | 281.6 | 45.2 : 47.3 : 7.5 | 51.1 | |
| Tris. | 476 | 365 | 258 | 1099 | 1428 | 1095 | 774 | 3297 | 51.6 | 39.6 | 28.0 | 119.2 | 43.3 : 33.2 : 23.5 | : 43.4 | 61.8 : 38.2 |
| Tetr. | 83 | 53 | 89 | 225 | 332 | 212 | 356 | 900 | 13.3 | 8.2 | 16.6 | 38.1 | 35.3 : 22.0 : 42.7 | 42.4 | |
| Pent. | 7 | 3 | 15 | 25 | 35 | 15 | 75 | 125 | | | | | | | |
| Hex. | — | — | 5 | 5 | — | — | 30 | 30 | | | | | | | |
| | | | | | 5321 | 5012 | 1817 | 12150 | 192.2 | 181.0 | 65.6 | 438.8 | 43.8 : 41.2 : 15.0 | : 48.2 | |
| **I-VI** | | | | | | | | | | | | | | | |
| Dis. | 6887 | 7166 | 1022 | 15075 | 13774 | 14332 | 2044 | 30150 | 130.6 | 135.8 | 19.4 | 285.8 | 45.7 : 47.5 : 6.8 | : 51.0 | |
| Tris. | 1785 | 1316 | 967 | 4068 | 5355 | 3948 | 2901 | 12204 | 50.6 | 37.5 | 27.5 | 115.7 | 43.9 : 32.4 : 23.7 | : 42.4 | 64.2 : 35.8 |
| Tetr. | 282 | 163 | 293 | 738 | 1128 | 652 | 1172 | 2952 | 12.1 | 6.7 | 13.9 | 32.7 | 37.0 : 20.7 : 42.3 | : 41.3 | |
| Pent. | 29 | 10 | 52 | 91 | 145 | 50 | 260 | 455 | | | | | | | |
| Hex. | 1 | 2 | 5 | 8 | 6 | 12 | 30 | 48 | | | | | | | |
| | 20408 | 18994 | 6407 | 45809 | | | | | 193.4 | 180.1 | 60.7 | 434.2 | 44.6 : 41.5 : 13.9 | : 48.2 | |

## XVI. WORD LENGTH

### Tris. and Polys. per 100 Lines (No. of Syllables)

|  | I | II | M | Total |  | I | II | M | Total |
|---|---|---|---|---|---|---|---|---|---|
| *Comus* | 30.9 | + 73.4 | + 19.8 | = 124.1 | *PL* I-II | 61.8 | + 44.1 | + 35.4 | = 141.3 |
| *PL* I | 65.2 | + 43.6 | + 34.9 | = 143.7 | III-IV | 58.5 | + 41.3 | + 35.8 | = 135.7 |
| II | 59.1 | + 44.4 | + 35.9 | = 139.4 | V-VI | 65.5 | + 42.3 | + 48.4 | = 156.2 |
| III | 65.4 | + 43.8 | + 40.4 | = 149.6 | VII-VIII | 75.0 | + 49.0 | + 50.9 | = 174.9 |
| IV | 54.0 | + 39.9 | + 32.8 | = 126.8 | IX-X | 61.7 | + 46.7 | + 43.4 | = 151.8 |
| V | 64.6 | + 45.1 | + 41.4 | = 151.1 | XI-XII | 57.1 | + 41.8 | + 35.4 | = 134.3 |
| VI | 66.4 | + 39.6 | + 55.3 | = 161.3 |  |  |  |  |  |
| VII | 68.9 | + 43.1 | + 46.1 | = 158.1 |  |  |  |  |  |
| VIII | 81.1 | + 54.8 | + 55.5 | = 191.4 |  |  |  |  |  |
| IX | 54.1 | + 41.4 | + 41.1 | = 136.5 |  |  |  |  |  |
| X | 70.0 | + 52.2 | + 46.0 | = 168.2 |  |  |  |  |  |
| XI | 58.8 | + 39.9 | + 32.3 | = 131.0 |  |  |  |  |  |
| XII | 55.1 | + 44.9 | + 39.6 | = 139.6 |  |  |  |  |  |
| *PR* I | 51.0 | + 41.8 | + 37.8 | = 130.6 | *PR* I-IV | 50.0 | + 53.9 | + 38.5 | = 142.5 |
| II | 38.7 | + 51.7 | + 41.3 | = 131.7 |  |  |  |  |  |
| III | 60.0 | + 66.3 | + 39.7 | = 166.0 |  |  |  |  |  |
| IV | 50.8 | + 55.7 | + 36.0 | = 142.5 |  |  |  |  |  |
| *SA* (A) | 63.9 | + 51.6 | + 39.7 | = 155.2 | *SA* (A-C) | 54.5 | + 56.8 | + 45.3 | = 156.5 |
| (B) | 56.1 | + 55.9 | + 52.0 | = 164.0 |  |  |  |  |  |
| (C) | 40.4 | + 64.5 | + 43.2 | = 148.1 |  |  |  |  |  |

*PL* (Gilbert's Rearrangement)

| | | | | |
|---|---|---|---|---|
| I | 60.2 | + 44.1 | + 35.9 | = 139.7 |
| II | 52.2 | + 34.0 | + 26.8 | = 112.9 |
| III | 56.6 | + 41.8 | + 40.9 | = 139.4 |
| IV | 64.4 | + 42.6 | + 45.7 | = 152.5 |
| V | 64.7 | + 44.3 | + 40.1 | = 149.1 |
| VI | 64.9 | + 47.8 | + 44.6 | = 157.3 |

# APPENDIX

## Gilbert's Chronological Rearrangement of *Paradise Lost*

GROUP I: IV. 268-85, 539-49; VIII. 457-520; IV. 8-31, 42-130, 356-94, 505-38; IX. 99-178; IV. 869-1015; X. 474-501; IX. 1067-1189; X. 720-908; III. 93-134, 203-10; XI. 193-369, 466-552; XII. 270-649.

GROUP II: X. 649-719; XI. 134-92, 423-65, 637-901; XII. 111-54, 260-69.

GROUP III: IV. 1-8, 32-41, 132-71, 205-68, 288-355, 408-504, 598-775, 549-97; V. 1-8, 11-25, 136-219; X. 909-1104.

GROUP IV: IV. 776-99 823-68; V. 694-714; VI. 44-98, 202-669; VII. 131-640; VIII. 204-456, 521-643; IX. 48-98, 179-1066.

GROUP V: I. 1-669; II. 629-48, 884-1055; III. 56-92, 418-742; IV. 172-204, 395-408, 799-822; V. 219-560, 561-76; VI. 894-912; VII. 40-130; VIII. 644-53; X. 1-228, 332-44; XI. 1-133, 370-442, 552-636; XII. 1-110, 155-260.

GROUP VI: I. 670-798; II. 1-520, 521-628, 648-884; III. 1-55, 135-202, 210-417; V. 8-11, 26-135, 577-693, 715-802, 803-907; VI. 1-43, 99-202; VI. 669-893; VII. 1-39; VIII. 1-204; IX. 1-47; X. 229-331, 345-414, 585-648, 414-473, 502-84.

# UNIVERSITY OF FLORIDA MONOGRAPHS

*Humanities*

No. 1: *Uncollected Letters of James Gates Percival*
Edited by Harry R. Warfel

No. 2: *Leigh Hunt's Autobiography: The Earliest Sketches*
Edited by Stephen F. Fogle

No. 3: *Pause Patterns in Elizabethan and Jacobean Drama*
By Ants Oras

No. 4: *Rhetoric and American Poetry of the Early National Period.* By Gordon E. Bigelow

No. 5: *The Background of The Princess Casamassima*
By W. H. Tilley

No. 6: *Indian Sculpture in the John and Mable Ringling Museum of Art.* By Roy C. Craven, Jr.

No. 7: *The Cestus. A Mask*
Edited by Thomas B. Stroup

No. 8: *Tamburlaine, Part I, and Its Audience*
By Frank B. Fieler

No. 9: *The Case of John Darrell: Minister and Exorcist.* By Corinne Holt Rickert

No. 10: *Reflections of the Civil War in Southern Humor*
By Wade H. Hall

No. 11: *Charles Dodgson, Semeiotician*
By Daniel F. Kirk

No. 12: *Three Middle English Religious Poems*
Edited by R. H. Bowers

No. 13: *The Existentialism of Miguel de Unamuno*
By José Huertas-Jourda

No. 14: *Four Spiritual Crises in Mid-Century American Fiction.* By Robert Detweiler

No. 15: *Style and Society in German Literary Expressionism.* By Egbert Krispyn

No. 16: *The Reach of Art: A Study in the Prosody of Pope*
By Jacob H. Adler

No. 17: *Malraux, Sartre, and Aragon as Political Novelists*
By Catharine Savage

No. 18: *Las Guerras Carlistas y el Reinado Isabelino en la Obra de Ramón del Valle-Inclán*
Por María Dolores Lado

No. 19: *Diderot's Vie de Sénèque: A Swan Song Revised.* By Douglas A. Bonneville

No. 20: *Blank Verse and Chronology in Milton.* By Ants Oras